Praise for Taming Me

"As Lucy's story unfolds, distance and a fear of humans are replaced by trust and a sense of belonging. With sharp insight, author Cathy Unruh lets us experience this changing world through Lucy's eyes. We learn the power of compassion to transform and come to understand that, in Lucy's world and in our own, miracles are possible."

Bryan Kortis, co-founder,
New York City's Neighborhood Cats

"Move over, Marley. *Taming Me* is poised to steal the hearts of animal fans everywhere. Not a cat lover? This feral feline, who narrates her own tale of survival, will turn you into one."

Margo Hammond, co-author, *Between the Covers:*
The Book Babes' Guide to a Woman's Reading Pleasures

"A romp through the mind of a fabulous feline and all her fun and life-changing adventures."

Rory Freedman, author, *Skinny Bitch*

"Delightful. As Lucy comes to know human kindness for the first time, her fear melts away, and she begins to love and trust her human parents—a captivating story about compassion and the connection that can exist between humans and other animals."

Gene Baur, author, *Farm Sanctuary:*
Changing Hearts and Minds About Animals and Food;
president and co-founder, Farm Sanctuary

"Wow. Cathy Unruh has captured the essence of the lives of feral (stray) cats in a charming and informative story. Readers will experience the joys, sadness and challenges Lucy faces in surviving and adapting to 'domesticated' life. A must read for every animal lover and an eye opener for those unfamiliar with feral cats. It is sure to melt any heart. I can't wait to read more of Lucy's adventures in the upcoming sequels!"

Myriam Parham, president, Florida Voices for Animals

"A fascinating story about how this special little island kitten overcame her life as a feral and learned to trust and blend into a new family. The book shows how animals share the same fears, emotions, love and acceptance that we humans do and how much our lives are enriched when we add an animal to our family. I look forward to reading more of Lucy's travels around the world."

Sherry Silk, executive director,
Humane Society of Tampa Bay

"You must come and join Lucy Miracle on her journey from being a feral kitten to a loved family member. Through Lucy's eyes you will share the good times and bad, and come away with a newfound appreciation for the struggle of feral cats everywhere. This is a beautifully written, fascinating tale of transformation that will leave you thankful that the world has people like the author and her family and friends in it."

Dennis McCullough, Hillsborough County
Florida Animal Services, retired

"A heartwarming and inspiring story of a feral cat, of those who loved her, and of the miracle they launched together on a tiny island in the Bahamas. The story, told by Lucy Miracle herself, will show you our world through the eyes of a helpless kitten who must learn to survive on her own, and to grow to trust and love the humans who share the island with her. Unruh's ability to write and think like a cat is astonishing. After reading *Taming Me*, your perception of cats and kittens will be forever changed. A 'must read' for anyone who has a kitten or a cat, any adult or child who will be entrusted with a pet of their own, or for anyone who simply wants to learn more about animals."

Jim MacDougald, president, International Council of the Tampa Bay Region

"Although a work of fiction, this book is in every way a true representation of the life of a stray kitten. A book that should not only be read, but also passed on to others for the messages it contains and the lessons offered. It emits an introspective look into a feline life that often goes unnoticed (much like the panhandlers on the streets you might pass on a daily basis). It encourages you to look inside of yourself and ask this question: 'What if the kitten I see near the dumpsters really needs my help?' *Taming Me* gives you instructions without lectures and hope for the future along with tools to use should you wish to reach out and help that stray cat or kitten you notice in your life."

Mary Anne Miller, founder and editor, Felinexpress.com

Taming Me

MEMOIR OF A CLEVER ISLAND CAT

Cathy Unruh

Taming Me: Memoir of a Clever Island Cat
Copyright © 2012 by Cathy Unruh

Published by

4244 Corporate Square
Naples, Florida 34104
Email: info@collagebooks.com
Tel: 800-565-0922
Fax: 239-643-7883
www.collagebooks.com

Although based on a true story, this is a work of fiction. All characters depicted, names used, and incidents portrayed in this novel are fictitious. No identification with actual persons is intended nor should be inferred. Any resemblance of the characters portrayed to actual persons, living or dead, is purely coincidental.

Trade Paperback ISBN: 978-0-938728-15-3
Hardcover ISBN: 978-0-938728-25-2
Library of Congress Control Number: 2012939934
Printed in the United States of America
First printing October, 2012

10 9 8 7 6 5 4 3 2 1

Taming Me is available at special quantity discounts for bulk purchases for educational needs, promotions, premiums and fundraising. For details contact the publisher, Collage Books Inc.

For Emily Sturman, who first suggested
that my story might be worth telling.

~ Lucy Miracle

Table of Contents

CHAPTER ONE

Feral Cat

We have just broken through a stand of bromeliads when we smell it: souring milk, tinged with salt. We charge forward, across an open patch of aging mulch. A discarded human food bag glitters in the last rays of the sun, beckoning us from the edge of the woods ahead. My mother is almost close enough to snag the enticing sack when she stops abruptly, her feet skidding and her head snapping backward. Her tail sags ominously, and she stands as though immobilized. I slow until I reach her, then nudge around her to look.

Shiny pictures of popcorn dance obscenely above a pair of legs sticking out of the bag. They are barely more than bone covered by wisps of fur. Their knees are planted in the dirt, their paw pads pointing skyward. A tail lies like a wilted worm between them, blanketed by dust. The chill afternoon wind travels up the tail, rippling the fur and filling the bag. It crackles open, releasing the rancid stench of death. Now I can see hip bones thrusting against fur, like tree roots straining upward through the grass. This is the first dead kitten I've seen. Tantalized by the smell of crumbs, he must have heaved himself inside a human food bag, but could not gather enough sustenance to crawl out and continue the hunt.

My mother turns away decisively, her bony shoulder brushing my whiskers, signaling me to follow. We walk toward the gumbo-limbo trees that cover the sand from beach to road, and pick up the smell of lightly rotting conch.

"Not that high!" A gravelly human voice yells just before the violent "*Whack!*" of a machete slicing through wood. And then a branch, its skin shredded and peeling like a fish under the claws of a heron, twists and tumbles downward, catching on other limbs as it falls. The limbs shudder and release the larger branch as it bobbles its way toward the sand, where it lands with a thud that echoes outward so that I feel the ripples beneath my paws. My mother and I sprint behind a nearby trunk.

"Get the lower branches, the smaller ones. We want to thin it out, not butcher it!" yells the gravelly voice. It is a male human, standing on the ground and shouting upwards into the tree, where a skinny young human is wrapped around the trunk like a vine, a foot planted on a branch, a leg and arm coiled around the center stalk, the other arm bent with the weight of the machete it holds.

"All right, okay," the skinny human calls to the one on the ground as he shimmies downward, machete flashing against the gumbo-limbo's oily leaves.

My mother brushes me with her tail, and we lope toward the road where the trees are thinner. A golf cart zooms by, its wheels threateningly close. The gush of air it leaves behind lifts my whiskers. My mother and I run now, deeper into the trees, away from the humans, away from the road.

I am new to this journey. Before my travels with my mother began, she scrounged alone for every edible morsel she could find. She would tuck my siblings and me away and set out on her foraging, leaving us mewing pitifully with our stomachs rumbling, under a tree or an abandoned building, sometimes on the lip of an overgrown, long-empty cistern, or beneath an unkempt bush. Thin and tired herself from our constant demands—not only to be fed, but to be sheltered and licked to sleep—she was nevertheless forced to scrabble for enough food to sustain all of us. A lizard in her belly, a bird, sometimes a scrap of the humans' leftover dinner or discarded lunch, meant enough milk to nurse us through another night.

I still crave her milk, although she is trying to wean me. It's not just the nourishment anymore. I know that it's time for me to find food for myself—my siblings have all set off on their own. It's my mother's company that I can't bear to part with. My whiskers practically touch her hind leg as we walk. The brush grows dense beneath the trees, and her body opens a path for me as we pick our way through.

My mother stops to sniff, flaring her nostrils. My nose twitches along with hers. The conch smells closer, but I can't see it—just fallen leaves and tree limbs, tangled in weeds, along with shreds of bark, crumpled and drying on the ground. A knobby root is just ahead, twisting through the underbrush, shoulder high. I run around my mother and launch myself upward onto the root. My claws catch a nub of wood, but I can't keep my grip and topple backward. I try again. I thrust my claws into the root just below the nub and hoist myself up, wobbling as I reach the top. I find a flat spot and curl my claws into the tree, gripping it tightly, aiming my face into the wind that carries the scent of conch. From my perch, I see patches of open ground, daylight flashing above them, but no conch.

"*Mrreow!*"

The cry escapes my mouth before I can stop it, as my mother bats my hindquarters. Her claws are out. They scrape the skin at the base of my fur. I wobble again in surprise and tumble off the root. My mother thrusts her face at mine. "Hsss!" she says. I lower my eyes and drop my chin, telling her that I know I've done wrong. It is dangerous to jump up where I might be seen. But I am so small, the temptation to find a higher view often overtakes me. My mother turns away and

starts to walk on, toward the conch. I trudge along behind her,
staying low.

We are close to where my littermates and I were born, near
a ledge of rocks where our island juts out into the ocean. The
edges of the rocks are smoothed by the surf that hurls itself onto
the narrow point. Across the water, a faded lighthouse stands
watch over an unused dock, crumbling into the sea. There are
not many humans here. Houses stand empty; sea grape trees
mix with gumbo-limbos and casuarinas on overgrown lots.

It was a sea grape tree that my mother selected as our
first shelter. Its heavy branches hung low and hugged the
sandy ground. Its fleshy leaves muffled her birthing moans and
shielded us from the chilly drizzle as she licked our bloody,
newborn bodies dry and offered us our first teat, a slow trickle
of her new-fallen milk, warm and teasing. We were as many
kittens as my mother had paws, jumbled in a tight, wriggling
clump. But the sea grape tree could not keep us safe. Hungry
egrets and herons consider newborn kittens a choice meal, and
the frenzied rats that rustle through the undergrowth might
have tried to nibble at us.

So my mother moved us—as she would do constantly until we were big enough to take care of ourselves—from the sea
grape tree to the many hiding places behind a huge, uninhab-
ited estate, including a shadowy space beneath concrete steps
that led down to the beach; the corner of the gazebo; the folds
of a fallen net on the tennis court; and the dark and dry utility
room whose door stood open just wide enough for my mother
to wedge through, a single kitten at a time dangling from her
mouth. Then she carried us from the estate to a spot just behind
the garbage cans across the narrow road; from the garbage cans
to the back deck of a wooden cottage on the beach; from the
cottage to some slowly rotting boards in a refuse pile along
the lane. Back and forth, back and forth my mother went,

grabbing us by the scruffs of our necks, carrying us through the inky night to our newest spot, never staying long enough in any single place for our scent to settle and entice a predator, or for any of the island's humans to learn our whereabouts.

My need to be close to her started then, before I could stand or see or hear, when my eyes were still closed and my ears remained pinned against my skull. She did her best to comfort us—as she does now, turning to touch my nose with hers before she plows ahead, letting me know that I am forgiven for my careless leap onto the root.

She always varied the order in which she carried us. She must have known that being the first or the last to travel was terrifying, for either way, you were left alone for many long, lonesome breaths, no ball of fur next to you as company and comfort, no heartbeat but your own. Our only sense of safety came from cuddling close to one another—you would have thought we were a single kitten, the way we curled into each other, paws tucked into tummies, faces under tails. But when my mother returned from her treks, her dusty smell announcing her arrival, her purr reassuring us that this was indeed our mother approaching, we separated frantically, searching for her milk, kneading at her belly to hasten its flow, sucking, sucking, drinking as much as she could offer us, and always wanting more.

"Poos-Poos!"

We stop in our tracks as a human calls out. We fling our bellies onto the ground, flattening our bodies beneath a fallen branch. Our ears stand up.

"Poos-Poos!"

I feel my mother relax. I do the same. The voice is calling in a friendly human tone, and we recognize it. It is female, hailing another cat. "There you are!" she calls, as the cat emerges from a hedge and runs straight to her. He is a tough, scrubby-haired male, the color of the evening sun. His territory is near the house where the woman stands chopping at a glistening, lifeless grouper on her deck—a house that is occupied more often than most of the others. The woman who lives there likes to fish. The tom used to sneak into her bushes and watch as she sliced up the fish, throwing their heads and bones into the wash of the waves along the sand. The tom would dart from the bushes and snatch a carcass before it could float away. The female human saw him doing this, but rather than chase him off her property, she started to throw the fish heads in his direction! Over many moons, the tom and the woman got so comfortable next to each other that she gave him a human name: Poos-Poos.

The tom reaches the steps that lead to the woman's deck and stops, his head angled upward as he eyes the grouper. "Halloo, my friend!" she says, tossing the grouper's head, lopped off just below the gills, onto the sidewalk. The tom crunches into it, not hurried, not hidden! He eats it right out there in the open, as the woman continues talking to him. "Not too many fish today," she says. "I couldn't stay out long—the seas are up a bit. I had Jeremy with me and he actually started to feel sick, so we came on in." She chuckles and shakes her head, still chopping.

I have watched this tom in action many times. My mother started taking my siblings and me to his territory as soon as we could walk that far on our own. She wanted us to learn from him because he is the oldest cat we know and has survived many dangers. He is a rare cat on our island for another reason: he has come to know a human well enough to begin to think of her property as safe. Very few cats feel so comfortable that they settle in on a human's lawn or porch. Rarer still is the cat who begins to see a human as a companion—and with good reason.

Our history on the island has been troubled and erratic.

Many of our ancestors were poisoned or taken out to sea and drowned. In fact, terrible things still happen. Some of the humans grumble that cats are a nuisance, and that there are too many of us. They don't like to see our scrawny bodies diving into the hedges as they drive their golf carts along the road; they don't like to watch us scampering out of garbage cans or running for cover when they walk by. "Those cats must have diseases," they'll say, or "What pests! They're worse than pigeons!"

It is especially daring and dangerous to hunt for table scraps around an outdoor eating area that is attached to a human's house, but that's exactly what we were doing when I heard humans talk about killing us with guns.

"Remember when Stonegood was on the island? He used to carry a shotgun in his golf club rack," chuckled a voice wafting through a window. "He'd see a cat crossing the road and boom! That'd be the end of that cat."

"He was a crack shot!" another voice exulted.

"Not everyone shot cats just for sport," said another. "Some people considered it the best way to keep the population under control. They thought it was more humane than poison."

"Maybe so, but some people just plain hate cats—like that reclusive weirdo Uberan," a slow, deep voice responded. "He'd love to kill them all." I'd heard other humans say similar things about this man.

By now I was quivering, my search for scraps forgotten with the horror of what I was hearing. My mother interrupted her own quest to nuzzle my neck. She wanted to comfort me, but she also wanted my littermates and me to learn. And we did. Fear became a natural consequence of our education.

I was mystified by this hatred for cats because our island's name is Cat Cay, and the picture the humans draw of it shows a cat on a key, the tiny metal tool that humans use to start their golf carts and lock up their houses when they leave the island

for long stretches. That picture is on signs all over the island: a
cat the color of night, his back curving upward as he balances
gracefully on a giant key. Why are we not revered and cared
for here?

There *are* occasional humans who pity us. They put out
plates of food and call, "Here, kitty, kitty," to let us know
that it's there. But those people are few, and they never stay
on the island for long. The humans here all come and go
unpredictably. And there is so much competition for the
food that we cannot depend on it. Instead, we hunt.

Turning away from the tom and his feast, my mother leads
me to a garbage can across from the female human's house.
I hide behind a fence as she jumps over it and into the can.
Garbage cans are obvious places to look. They hold plastic
trash bags, filled in cooking and eating rooms, waiting to be
picked up by island workers. I hear my mother's claws ripping
through a bag and the rattle of empty soda cans. My nose is
alert for any hint of dinner: maybe a blob of soggy cereal, or
a tuna can that still contains a morsel, perhaps a fragment of
lobster or conch. Maybe my mother will find a real meal: half
a bowl of macaroni, a chunk of moldy cheese, stale remnants
of a loaf of bread. But she emerges empty-mouthed, and I feel
my stomach lurch like the beak of a frustrated heron watching
a guppy swim away.

We don't bother to stop at the next can we come to; it's
filled with palm fronds and building materials. We travel
through a palm tree thicket, searching for a coconut that has
cracked open after falling hard enough on the ground. A
coconut's sweet clear milk and fleshy meat are a special treat,
clean and delicious. But the only coconuts we find are whole,
tough and unblemished by their tumble from the trees. We
trudge onward toward the rotting conch.

The sun has fallen behind the ocean by the time we find

the source of the smell: a small tower of conch shells sits atop an open ridge of coral rock lining the shore. We run to the shells and begin to paw, upending them. They have been emptied by humans and are fairly fresh; splinters of chewy conch meat still cling to their insides. I gnaw the slivers of conch loose and swallow them. I lick at the drops of conch juice mixed with seawater that have settled into the basin of the shell. My mother and I work our way through the entire pile, lapping and chewing. When we are done, I am exhausted.

I lie down on the coral rock, ignoring its jagged edges. The air gusting in from over the sea feels surprisingly warm and smells deliciously of fish. But my mother refuses to join me in a nap out here in the open. She sets off for the trees. I force myself to get up and follow. My mother chooses a sea grape tree to settle under. While she bathes, I put my head on my paws and watch, willing myself to stay awake. I want to snuggle next to her as soon as she rests. I yearn for her warmth.

I am a scrawny thing, thinner than any of my littermates— I have not grown into my age. Born in the moist dense heat of summer, I have now been alive long enough for the days to shorten and go dry. I would likely perish in the sudden chill without my mother—if hunger didn't fell me first. I think of the kitten in the popcorn bag and shiver. I creep closer to my mother. My body looks so much like hers: the color of sand on my underbelly, shoulders, and legs, with dirt-colored patches on my back and feet, accented by stripes the color of the island roads—blacktop, they call it—winding around and down my tail like a snake. I wonder if my face resembles hers. Fur the color of cinders outlines her eyes and swoops upward toward the whiskers in her ears. She has a beautiful straight ear, the solid color of a ripening coconut, and a crooked ear, dark at the bottom and pale at the tip. A patch shaped like a sand dollar sits on her cheek. I reach up and lick the patch, purring. My mother licks me back. She lies down, and I nuzzle against her, searching for a teat. She pushes me away. I persist, nestling in against her heart. I barely hear a beat before I am asleep.

My mother is already stirring when the familiar evening rustle awakens me: hermit crabs, lizards and rats combing the underbrush. We resume our walk, past a stand of buttonwood trees and toward one of the scaevola hedges that grow rampant on our island. The hedges are thick; the wide leaves of the scaevola look almost knotted, the way they loop together. The bushes' tangled spines offer shelter to all sorts of creatures—bugs, worms, tiny soft-shelled crabs—and the predators who hunt them, especially after dark.

We crawl beneath the scaevola, and I crouch beside my mother, completely still. Our eyes search the ground for the scamper of lizards tracking bugs, and then—pounce! A lizard hunting for his own food becomes ours, pinned beneath my mother's agile paw. She bats him into unconsciousness and shares him with me, but he is big enough for only a couple of bites between us. Nearby, a rat scurries along the ground. Rats are far too quick for a kitten to even think of tackling, so I wait once again while my mother chases him. But he is a cunning creature, dodging from side to side, weaving in and out of gaps in the scaevola vines, spaces too small for my mother. She persists, picking up his trail each time he emerges and hoping to hound him until he slows with fatigue, but he finally evades her by scurrying up a skinny stretch of scaevola spine and disappearing into its leaves.

We abandon the scaevola and slog onward through casuarina branches and palm fronds downed by the winter winds. A splotchy female passes us without a glance, her tail high, intent on her own mission. We hear a flutter above us and look up; a mourning dove settles in the nook of a tall branch. He looks small enough for my mother to handle, but she is too drained to attempt the climb up the tree.

Birds are difficult prey, but when she had a ravenous litter of mouths to feed, my mother was forced to try. She would lie in wait beneath a tree until the bananaquit or swallow flittering above would forget her presence and begin to swoop and dive toward the ground. Then—pounce! When she was lucky, my mother would time it just right, leaping onto the delicate bird and delivering a death bite to the throat before laying the limp and quivering body at our paws.

Woodpeckers sometimes made for an easier meal. A woodpecker could be so intent on pounding his beak into a tree that he wouldn't see or hear my mother sneak up behind him. She would sink her teeth into the nape of his neck just as the bird thrust backward to gather momentum for another peck.

My mother had an especially tough time catching mockingbirds. Their shadowy coloring makes it easy for them to hide in the crooks of trees. And they can fool you: a mockingbird knows how to change his song so that he sounds like a sparrow, or a robin, or many of the other birds on our island. My mother would think she was climbing a tree trunk after a sparrow and then—surprise! She'd come upon a fat, fearless mockingbird instead, willing to lunge at a cat as quickly as at a lizard, swooping down to peck her tail or bite her ear.

"All right, all right, okay." A human voice, male!

We dash for cover in a thicket of railroad vine. Footsteps tromp through the woods, straight at us. My mother drapes a leg over my shoulders, telling me not to move. I smell mud and yeast, as the footsteps get closer.

Then, a throatier male voice: "...have to open the commissary early tomorrow, so we'd better not party too hard!"

Leaves crunch as the footsteps get closer. My mother's leg grows tense and tight across my back. I press my chin hard into the ground. A branch breaks, from somewhere behind my head, snapped from a tree. Now it sweeps the ground, back and forth, back and forth, pushing fallen leaves and empty shells— probably even hermit crabs—out of its way. The sweeping noise comes closer, brisker, as the voices get louder.

"You bring any tunes?"

"No, Jackson said he'd be along with some."

"Hope Jezzie comes too. Now there's a serious fox!"

Laughter. The sweeping and the footsteps and the voices feel like they are almost on our tails. My mother's leg trembles.

More laughter. "All right, okay!"

Bottles clink against each other, practically over our heads. Island workers, out for an evening beer. My mother presses her paw into me, signaling. She rises to her feet and flees off into the trees, fast and smooth like a heron taking flight.

"Yo!" A human, startled, stops. The sweeping sound stops. I leap up and rush after my mother as fast as I can, not looking back. The voices resume. "Just a couple of cats," I hear one say, before they dim and fade into the distant crash of waves against coral.

My mother is waiting for me at the next stand of trees. I collapse beside her, panting, my chest heaving. Her eyes sweep the area around us, searching. She waits for me to calm, then meows for me to follow her. We travel toward the commissary, where we might find some particularly tasty trash. We often lie in wait outside the store, watching humans walk in with money and come out with bags full of food.

Money is what humans need to live on our island. They talk of it often. Apparently, money is even better than meals, because the humans trade it not only for food, but for many other things as well. They turn money into houses, golf carts, boats and clothes, and they give money to other humans, so that they will take care of all of these things for them. The humans who take care of things are called employees, or workers. They are usually the darkest ones and are known as Bahamians. They speak of being born on other islands near here where their families still live—islands that are bigger than our small spit of land. The humans who give money to the workers live in the big houses that line the main roads. Their skins can look as pale as sand, or like tree bark, coral rock—even the insides of conch shells, when they stay out in the midday sun too long.

The Bahamians are the most likely to feed us, throwing leftovers from their porches in the employees' village or through the doors of the restaurant kitchen. But we do not allow ourselves to trust them either. The same night that I heard about Stonegood and shotguns, I learned about something called bounty.

"Some of those Bahamians are pretty good at capturing cats," a voice chimed in from beyond the open window. "They get a lot of practice with chickens."

"Yeah, remember that time we offered a bounty for any cat, dead or alive?"

"We got a lot of them that time. Can't blame the Bahamians for wanting a little extra money to send home to the family."

"How much was the bounty?" a new voice asked.

"Twenty-five bucks a head, if I remember correctly," came the answer.

Money, in exchange for our lives.

Weary of walking, I nudge my mother's leg. "Mrreeow," I plead, asking her to stop with me and rest.

"Mreow," she answers, in her throaty rumble that is as much a purr as a meow. She scans our surroundings for a safe spot and leads me toward an abandoned, doorless shed where many island animals gather to sleep in safety. Splintering boards, barely held on by corroded nails, hang down from its exterior. I smell feathers as we approach. Inside the shed, shelves line the walls. Chickens are roosting for the night between rusting tools, greasy rags, and small cans with dried paint drizzling down their sides.

As we walk in, a hen, squatting on a thin but sturdy board, flares her wings and covers her chicks—more chicks than my mother and I have paws put together. I hop up on the board to say hello. On the back edge rests a pile of nails. My front paw kicks into the pile as I skid to a stop. The nails clatter off the board, embarrassing me and setting the chicks into a frenzy.

With a feeble "meow" I try to explain that the board must have been too slippery, but the chicks do not understand me. "Cheep, cheep, cheep, cheep, *cheep!*" they cry, a chorus of unsettled chirps, their tiny webbed feet scrambling, their little wings flapping. The hen stretches her wingspread and the chicks rustle tightly together beneath it. I extend my nose toward the hen's beak in apology, but she opens it and screeches: "*Bok, bok, bok bok...BOK!*" My mother reaches out and swats me, ordering me off the board. I jump down. The hen settles, every chick covered by her wing feathers. She blinks furiously, tracking me with her bobbing, shiny eyes, as I turn to follow my mother, who raises her tail, stiff and annoyed. The other chickens barely open their eyes, apparently unfazed by my noisy accident. They are not afraid of us.

From early on, my littermates and I learned never to hunt the chickens and turkeys that roam the island as we do. Although their chicks move slowly and would be effortless to catch, a mother hen will ferociously protect her young. We once watched a dog charge a hen, galloping straight at her and the trail of chicks she led. Unafraid, the hen flew at the dog, flapping and squawking—almost close enough to peck his eyes out—before the dog finally turned tail and ran.

I remember that now, sheepishly tailing my mother. I'm glad that I have not upset the other chickens in the shed by trying to say hello. After many years of coexisting on the island, cats, chickens, roosters, and turkeys have all learned to live together in peace, often sleeping in the same space and eating the same food, although the fowl find more plentiful sustenance. They can rake through the dirt with their pointy feet, turning up bugs and worms. They also forage through the humans' building refuse—rotting planks, mahogany beams, crumbling window shutters—for termites. When the humans trim trees and chop up the branches, the chickens and turkeys feast on hordes of insects dislocated from their perches and forced to run for refuge along the ground.

My mother walks up to the solitary rooster keeping watch over his flock. She rubs her body against his, sharing her scent and reassuring him of our bond. He pecks at her cheek, one light jab, his comb jiggling in greeting.

We walk to the back corner of the shed and paw at a pile of rags, spreading them out to cover the cracking floorboards. The rags smell of oil and yet, they are a welcome cushion against the wood as we lie down. My mother turns her back to me, but doesn't move away as I settle one hip into her haunches.

I look around. There is a turkey hen on a high shelf, roosting with a pair of chicks. There are no peacocks in the sleeping shed. They prefer open trees and roofs where they can feel the air in their feathers. We have the same respect for peafowl as we do for chickens and turkeys. They even sound like us. The cry of a peacock, tail fully splayed as it calls for a mate, is the same as the loud mournful meow of a cat. The peahens hide their young so well that it is rare to stumble upon their chicks or eggs, but we wouldn't hunt them anyway. Outside, the wind picks up, banging the loose boards against the walls. The wooden thumping soothes me—a reminder that I am safely inside a shelter, surrounded by friends, with some food in my belly and my mother beside me. I purr, turn myself around, and begin to wash her face. I lap at her whiskers, her nose, her forehead. She closes her eyes and purrs beneath my tongue. How long will she tolerate me and my neediness, I wonder, before she forces me to go away and grow up, as all kittens are expected to do? I suspect that I am a burden to her, yet I am terrified to venture off alone. I lack the boldness of my larger siblings, who touched my mother's nose in farewell and left to hunt on their own.

The blustery weather outside is not enough to threaten us, but even the elements can conspire against cats. In this, we are surely soul mates with the chickens, turkeys and peafowl, all of us seeking shelter from the whims of nature. Our narrow island is open to gales off the sea, which can whip briskly enough to send waves down our fur, even strongly enough to make it impossible for a small cat to walk. We travel low when we feel the wind picking up, slouching along the ground until we can take cover beneath a building or a tree, against a fence or a large rock. Sometimes the wind is a warning of worse weather to come, like the rains that can hammer us in the hot late afternoons, hard and fast, creating pools of water that block our escape routes to favorite hiding places. And when the wind is accompanied by a deep grumble from out over the ocean, we dash for cover as quickly as possible, before the sky starts shooting hot light and making cracking sounds that seem to shake the island, sometimes sending tree branches crashing to the ground below.

Humans sometimes tell tales of weather unlike anything I have seen so far, even in the worst of storms. They call this weather "hurricane," and when humans think a hurricane is coming, there's a great scurrying about, as they fill up planes and boats and flee the island. They say a hurricane can send coconuts hurtling through the air like deadly rocks, and topple trees as though they are no sturdier than whiskers. They say the winds and rains of a hurricane can send the roof of a human house flying, crack open its glass windows, even lift its walls right off the ground.

"Remember '92?" I heard during such a human conversation. "It was like some kind of giant had just walked up and down the island, tromping on houses and flattening everything."

"No kidding. It looked like most of the Cay was a dumping ground: building materials, trashed trees, uprooted foliage everywhere."

A Bahamian said that during the storm, a co-worker tied himself to a giant gumbo-limbo tree and hung onto its trunk until the winds moved on, sparing the tree—and him.

Cats might have an advantage over humans during vicious weather, if we sense it coming quickly enough to seek shelter. We can crawl down into old, abandoned concrete cisterns, even into heavy metal pipes and conduit, and wait out the storm safely below ground. Cats who don't get to shelter in time, though, might be picked up by the wind and blown away with the buildings and tree limbs, or drowned in the rains that turn low lying areas into dangerous ponds.

Temperamental weather, incessant hunger, humans who want to hurt me…I pant as I imagine facing these perils alone. I feel my insides knot up like a worm on cold cement. I lick my mother's eyelids and settle in against her to sleep.

A light nip on my ear is a reminder not to waste the protection of night. I wake and stretch, extending my forelegs as far as they will go. They reach from the tip of my mother's ear to the base of her neck. I rub against her as I stand, a reminder of my affection. The chickens and turkeys do not awaken as we leave the shed. Even the rooster has flown up onto a shelf and allowed himself to doze.

We take the beach route to the commissary, following the shore and avoiding the houses. We pass a pair of cats heading into the hedges that line the outer edge of a gigantic lawn. I stare until they disappear; they share markings like my mother and me. A humongous hard-shell crab scampers across the sand, heading for the water. His pincers are bigger than my legs.

The aroma of slaughtered fish signals that we are nearing the marina. The smell is a torture to us. It comes from the cleaning station on the nearest dock, where humans cut up their fish, and it means *piles* of food nearby, yet out of our reach. We dare not venture there, out in the open with humans and no place to hide. We do not even have a chance at the parts of the fish that humans consider to be garbage—they toss those pieces into the water, where rays and sharks circle, anticipating the banquet. Pelicans and sea gulls plunge down and snatch up pieces of skin, tails, fins and eyeballs. Even now, in the night, when remnants of fish might remain on the chopping blocks, we dare not walk that way. Golf carts drive up and down the dock without warning, carrying humans out for a sightseeing drive, or on their way to a boat or the gas pump that stands at the end of the pier.

This is a dangerous region. All the humans seem to converge at the marina: the workers; the residents who come and go; the strangers who chug in on noisy boats, jump onto the wooden dock and wander the island for a while, eating at the restaurant or turning money into food at the commissary. Nonetheless, a few bold cats have declared this their territory. They emerge from beneath the buildings at sunrise to snatch scraps tossed from the restaurant kitchen toward the peacocks and peahens that fly down from the rooftops to eat. They dart onto the restaurant porch to catch crumbs fallen from the tables, or tidbits tossed at them. "Here, kitty, kitties," a diner will say, a chunk of fried conch in her outstretched hand. "Come here, kitty, kitties."

The cats will edge toward the diner's table, stopping behind a chair or under an unoccupied table nearby. "Won't you come any closer?" the diner asks. The cats do not. They know that any human who reaches out might be trying to capture or harm them rather than offering food or a tender touch. So they welcome the snippets that diners throw on the floor, but dodge the hands that feed them.

"Come on…you can have some conch if you'd like." The cats remain still and resolute, eyes staring at the conch, waiting. Experience has taught them what will happen next.

"I think if you're going to give it to them, you should just give it to them," says the diner's companion. "They're obviously not going to walk up and get it."

"I just wanted to try and pet one," says the diner with a sigh. She lobs the piece of conch at the cats, and then another and another, until each cat has a morsel of his own.

My mother and I leave the beach, avoiding the marina, and dash from bush to bush until we reach our destination: the several large trash cans that stand just up the hill, across the road from the store. But we are too late. The cans are empty. The trash bags are gone, probably taken away while we slept in the shed. Crestfallen, I hang my head and slump down onto my paws. Anguish overwhelms my hunger. It was my need to rest that delayed our arrival here. I whimper a short mournful plea for my mother's forgiveness. She noses my neck, telling me to get up and keep going; ravenous cats cannot rest.

My skin begins to long for relief along with my stomach as we brave a cold open stretch beyond the hill. Needles of discarded Christmas trees and strands of tinsel whip briskly through the air. We sneak along a fence that surrounds a pile of golf carts, their tires gone, their steering wheels broken off, their dented and corroded frames stacked together like deformed and broken shells. On the back seat of one cart, a pale cat sleeps, her fur blending with the seat cushion.

We head back toward where I was born, sniffing, our eyes scouring the sides of the road. We risk encounters with humans here, but we may find uneaten morsels tossed aside while they are out walking or riding, or food that has fallen off the garbage wagon, making its way to the burn pile at a distant end of the island. We eye the humans' houses for signs of habitation and the possibility of trash.

The first house we pass is a huge, sunny estate that straddles the road—unused tennis court and empty cistern on one side, main house, guest cottages, and utility buildings on the other. We hunch down, leave the roadside and slink along its fence. We know a spot just behind a shed where the house's workers sometimes throw out scraps; and even if there is no meal waiting, the hunting is good in the vegetation at the back of the property. We have found lots of lizards there, and even an occasional snake. I am scared of snakes, the way they thrust their pointy heads into the air and aim their wicked tongues my way, flicking them in and out and hissing like a demented angry cat. But my mother knows how to catch a snake, sneaking up from behind and chomping into it just beyond the head before it even senses her coming.

Forklifts, a tractor, and golf carts sit near the shed. We skirt from machine to machine, hiding beneath them while we check for humans. When we reach the grass just behind the shed, we halt, astonished. My mother and I look at each other, eyes wide, ears perked up. Can we believe what we are smelling?

The odor of fresh, juicy tuna fish floats heavily in the air. Not the faint whiff of a bite of tuna fish—no! This could be an entire fish, maybe more. The scent is so strong it seems to burden the wind as it drifts toward us. I lose the scent of trees, rats, lizards, crabs, leaves—my nose picks up nothing but the smell of tuna. It seems to sit on my whiskers. My mother and I confirm with a fast glance that our noses agree, and then we run toward the smell, suddenly heedless of danger, driven only by our stomachs, following the scent to its source: an open bowl brimming with skinless, oily tuna.

The bowl sits inside some sort of open wire contraption, not very wide, but plenty big enough to hold my mother and me. She dashes into it. I race right behind her, inside the wire box just a breath later, my tail barely through its opening as my mother lowers her mouth for the first succulent bite. A cold, jarring "slam!" rocks the box. It is a noise I've never heard before, the sickening rasp of metal locking on metal, but I know what it is: it is the sound of capture.

My mother goes berserk. She leaps straight up and flings herself around in the air, upending the tuna bowl and crashing her head into the bars of our cage, ears flattened against her skull, claws flung out as far as they will go, lips back in a snarl, as the most terrifying shriek I've ever heard hurtles out of her mouth. She is pure fear, mindless desperation, as she throws herself again and again around the cage, banging her head into it on every side, top and bottom, screaming and clawing and crying—while I cower in one tiny corner, paw pads clutching onto wire, making myself as small as I can, my heart pounding so forcefully that I can barely draw a breath, my own fear horribly magnified by the sight of my mother, on whom I depend so completely, going out of her mind with terror.

Eventually she tires, exhausted by her futile attempts to escape. She huddles down beside me, hunched on her paws as I am, and together we stare out at the evening, the reality of our situation settling on us like the dark: we are trapped.

And then, the sound of a golf cart pulling into the driveway. I scrunch as close to my mother as I can, trying to blend into her and the night, and to become invisible. Humans emerge and walk toward us. A pair of females, talking. My mother hisses, the sound of a snake about to attack, as a woman bends down toward our prison. "Well hello kitties—two of you! Look," she says, "it's a mommy and her little one."

"Oh, how precious!" the other woman exclaims, lowering her face toward us, as my mother hisses and hisses, trying to back up but finding no room. "Aren't they cute?" the woman asks, as she grabs for the top of our trap and picks it up. She carries us toward the golf cart, which sends my mother into another frenzy. She pitches her body back and forth, back and forth, against the bars of the trap, again to no avail. "Now calm down, kitty," is the woman's response as she grapples with the rollicking trap, refusing to let go.

They put us on the back seat of the golf cart and cover our cage with a cloth, so that we cannot see where we are going as the cart backs up. I take strange comfort in the sudden, complete darkness underneath the cloth, and plaster my body against my mother's.

When the cart comes to a stop, we hear more voices, both human and cat. The human voices are male, deep and calm, but the cats' are a mangle of sounds. They are as terrified as we are, wailing, hissing, screeching. When the women take the cloth off our trap, we see why: other traps just like ours are lined up on the ground, each of them holding an island cat. The men are moving among the cages, looking in. "This one's already been done," says one of the men about a big, angry, cloud-colored tom—and amazingly, the man unlatches the door of his trap, letting the male cat gallop off through the grass, long muscles bulging with the ferocity of his run.

The women place our cage alongside the others. We tumble with its movement, grabbing at the wire floor.

"This one, too," says one of the women about the calico in the cage next to us, "although her notch is awfully small. Do you think that's really a notch, or just an injury?" she asks her companion.

The other woman squats down near the cage and peers in.

"That's definitely a notch," she answers, "but they didn't make it very big."

And with that, the other woman opens the door of the cage. The calico shrinks back into the corner, unsure whether this is freedom or a new threat. "Come on, kitty, kitty, go back home," the woman coaxes. She upends the cage slightly, the angle causing the cat to slide toward the open door. The calico makes a run for it, vanishing into the night.

When the men get to our cage, I cringe, flattening myself into the corner. "This one looks pretty small," one of the men says, staring in at me.

"She does," answers the other man, stooping down to get a closer look. "Hard to tell the age of these cats, some of them get so little to eat."

"Do you think she's big enough?"

"Yes, she'll probably make it. Let's take her in. If we don't, she'll have twenty kittens before we get to her next year. Time to get started?"

The first man nods yes, reaching into his pocket. He pulls out a long, slim, tube shimmering with fluid, and squats next to our cage. As his hand reaches toward my mother, she screams: one last, long despairing screech. A needle—thinner and sharper than the end of a cat fang—jabs hard into my mother's haunches. Her shriek shrivels into a moan, and my mother crumples like a bag of sand being emptied onto the beach.

Finally, I cry, wrenched out of my petrified silence by despair. The man's hand is coming at me and there is no way to escape it. I crush my body against the cruel metal bars of the cage, shaking, and feel the spike thrust into my hindquarters and then a quick vicious sting. I am half aware of my head lolling down onto the floor of the cage as my cry fades like the final unanswered yowl of a peacock, collapsing its tail in defeat. I, too, am turning to sand, my consciousness spilling into nothingness as I make one last, futile attempt to move toward my mother, and then I am gone.

CHAPTER TWO

Captured Cat

Something soft and warm is being wrapped around me. I feel it as though from far away, as though I am in a treetop and it is happening to some other cat stretched out on the ground below me, and then I fall back into sleep.

When I surface again, I hear a hum, like some kind of machine; a door opens and shuts, its mechanical click echoing close to me. My wrapping is removed and a new one is placed around me, freshly warmed. I think my fur is wet. Someone is standing over me. "She is shivering!" says a Bahamian voice, deep and female.

"Yes," answers another female voice, lighter and softer, harder to hear through the fog in my head. "Her body temperature is way too low. We need to get her warmed up, or she's not going to survive." Another wrapping now encircles me, covering everything but my nose and eyes. I feel a slight soreness as the wrapping touches my ear.

"Could you please put some more towels in the dryer, Ginger?" the lighter voice asks.

I am in the sun. I can feel it hot on my face, but I am not outside. I am lying on something as soft as the sponge grass I love to roll in, and the intense afternoon rays reach me through the glass it rests against. I force my eyelids to open. A blink. Another. I see walls around me. Something is rubbing me, ruffling, then smoothing, my fur. Hunger claws at my stomach, like the pincers of a hermit crab climbing into an abandoned shell. I cannot help the hunger. I cannot lift my head. It has grown too heavy for my neck. I doze again.

Ouch! I feel something being pulled out of my body—something thin, but heavy. When it is all the way out, I hear a man's voice. "Just a couple of degrees below normal now," he says. "Not bad. She'll probably make it." I have heard this man say this before. I shiver, but not from cold. I struggle to raise my head and cannot.

"How old do you think she is?" asks another voice, this one a vaguely familiar female.

The man pulls back my mouth and runs his fingers over my gums. "I don't know, maybe three months, maybe five," he says. "She's so malnourished it's hard to say."

I clench my teeth together, feebly, but his fingers are gone.

I am lying on my back, in the grip of human hands, too weak to resist. There is a face right in front of me, a human face. Its nose is almost touching my nose. Its eyes look damp as they stare intently into mine, which I try desperately to hold open against the weight of my weariness.

"Come on, little girl," a voice whispers, and I struggle to focus, to put a face with the voice that I recognize, the voice of the woman who was wrapping me, warming me. I feel her human breath, thick on my whiskers. "Come on, you can make it. Please let her make it, God. If you'll just live, little girl, I will name you Miracle."

Warm milk! It's dropping against my mouth, dampening my whiskers, rousing me to try to suck. I open my mouth. The milk is dripping out of something skinny and hard, much harder than my mother's teat. I can't quite suck at it, so I simply swallow. I get some of the milk down my throat, and some of it slithers down my chin. It doesn't taste like my mother's milk; it's thinner and not as sweet, but it warms my throat and then my tummy.

This time, I am awake long enough to focus on the woman's face. It is pale with dark eyes. "Come on, little girl, drink as much as you can," the woman urges. She is still keeping me warm. But instead of wrapping me in heated cloths, she is holding me in the warmth of the sun as she feeds me. I am hungry, but I cannot stay awake to get my fill. I am on my back again in the woman's lap, resting on her thighs. The back of my head is on her knees. My legs are splayed open, as though they had gone limp with pleasure while I slept. The woman is wiping my belly with something soft, damp and sweet-smelling, gently going over it again and again.

My belly doesn't feel like it used to; something is different about it. I try to focus on the sensation of the wiping. I concentrate on the cloth, moving from my shoulders toward my hind legs. Then I realize what is strange about my belly: there's a bare patch of skin on it! The fur is gone, and the skin feels tighter than it used to, as though it has shrunk. The woman washes this bare spot repeatedly, gently, and then works her way over my fur, up my legs. "Little Miracle," she purrs at me in her human voice, and it's a soft rumble from deep in her throat, almost like a cat's. "My little Miracle."

By the time the damp, sweet cloth reaches my paws, I am fully awake for the first time since my capture—but where is my mother? I roll my head from side to side, looking. She is not here, in this strange space with this unknown human touching me!

I flex my paws, extend my claws, and study the woman's face, wondering where to scratch her. It will be a long drop from her lap to the floor, and I am on my back. Will I be able to right myself and get away?

The woman moves the cloth to my face, washing my whiskers. It tickles my nose and travels toward my eyes. I close them reflexively, and beneath the rhythm of the soft, damp strokes, I fall asleep again.

"Knock, knock!"

A human head pokes through a door across from me. "Anybody home?" The smells of grass and seaweed drift in.

"Just a minute!" The shout comes from behind a wall.

The man at the door steps through it and moves closer to me.

I am inside a human house, confined to a small cage. When I back up against it, as far from the human as I can get, the cage feels soft, not hard like the metal one in which I was captured.

"Oh, hi Larry!" says the familiar woman, walking in. "How are you?"

"Good, good," says the human at the door. "I've come by to see how our patient is doing." He eyes me.

"I think she's coming along!" says the woman. "She's alert, and she's been eating on her own for a couple of days now."

"Great!" says the man. "Mind if I take a peek?"

"Not at all." The woman walks toward me, leading the man. I try to back up further, scrunching my body against the cage, which sits on a long soft couch beside a giant window. I feel sunshine on my fur, filtering through the glass. Despite its warmth, I shiver. I hear the man's voice again, this time in my head. "Looks like she's coming along," his voice is saying. I tremble from nose to tail as he bends down and peers into my cage. I meet his eyes briefly. They are big, intense. I turn my head away, ducking it down, trying to tuck it into my neck. I flatten my ears.

"She looks good," the man says. "A little bit dirty, still, but she's fully conscious."

"Oh, yes!" the woman laughs. "Fully conscious and fully full! She practically attacked her food once she woke up."

I bristle a bit. My cage contains a small bowl of moist, delicious food that tastes like mashed fresh fish and a smaller bowl of the thin, bland milk. The first time the woman set the bowls inside my cage, I did not attack. Far from it. I remembered the smell of tuna that lured my mother and me into the trap. I remembered hearing humans talk about the time they left open containers of sweet gooey liquid all over the island. Naturally, the starving cats lapped it up, not realizing that it was poison. And this food was from a human who had captured me and locked me up! So at first I took only tentative bites.

But the food tasted so good, and I was so hungry that—it's true—I could not restrain myself. I opened my mouth as wide as I could, picking up as much food with my tongue as it would hold, barely pausing to chew, swallowing as quickly as my throat allowed. I felt scared that the meal would be snatched away before I could finish it, even while I was fearful of what might happen to me because I was eating it. But when I had emptied the bowls, I felt fine.

"Well, that's a good sign," says the man. "She's probably been hungry for a long, long time."

"Not anymore!" says the woman. "Today, she hasn't even finished the food I've given her, although it's a second helping."

I twist my head and steal a glance at the bowls. They are both half full. I cannot hold all the food and milk that the woman gives me. After I lap up what's in the bowls, she fills them again and again.

"And we're working on the dirty part," continues the woman. "I'm using baby wipes, and she seems to really enjoy them. But she's been out there for a long time and was just crusted with grime."

"Too weak to bathe herself," says the man. "She'll come around. How's she doing with that little litter box?"

"Great!" says the woman. "She took right to it. We haven't had any messes anywhere but in the sand."

The sand is the only place to relieve myself in here. I squat in it when I need to, avoiding the bowls and the small cloth that I nap on.

"Well, it all sounds good to me," says the man, standing up. "Glad she's making out okay. What are you going to do with her?"

"I don't know. We haven't gotten that far," answers the woman. "One day at a time."

"How long are you here?" asks the man.

"We're hoping to stay for a couple of weeks," the woman answers.

"Well, my tour of duty is up on Tuesday. Let Mandy and me know if there's anything we can do for you."

"Thanks. You guys have been great," says the woman. She walks the man toward the door. "So how does a medical doctor learn to operate on cats, anyway?"

"If I hadn't learned to help these cats, Mandy would have had *me* snipped," he chortles.

The woman laughs too. "Well, thanks for flying in the vet. I'm glad he could show you the ropes!" she says. "And I really appreciate him making this special trip to the island to help us out. I definitely want this to become a regular practice. Maybe my vet from home can come help us next year." She goes outside with the man to his golf cart. I hop up on my box of sand to see the edge of its roof, barely visible through the glass in the door.

A nose is pressed up tight to my cage. I'm just coming out of a nap, and I back away from it, astonished. It is a cat's nose—dark with a pale tip, cool and damp, sniffing. The cat that it belongs to is a long, slender male, dark as a moonless sky, his whiskers and chest the sharp clean color of a coconut's meat. He is muscular and his fur is sleek and shiny. As he sidles along the side of my cage, moving toward my nest in the cloth, the bell that he wears on a collar around his neck tinkles lightly. His nose twitches, and he opens his mouth a bit to better inhale my scent.

My heart pounds, and I flatten my ears back against my head, signaling to him that I am ready to defend myself. No other cat besides my mother and my littermates has ever been this close to me, and I am unsure how to act with this stranger, but he seems more curious than aggressive. He lowers his body to match mine, sinking down on his paws in an unthreatening stance. I've seen my mother touch noses with cats who shrank down to her level—a sign of trust—but I don't know this cat or what to make of him. Am I on his territory?

"Mrreow," the cat says, his eyes wide and his voice lilting up with the inflection that asks, "Who are you?"

I'm trying to figure out how to react to him when I'm startled by the jingle of another bell. The sofa cushion sags with the weight of a different cat as he leaps up beside me. This one is a deep night color all over. He's slightly heavier than the first cat, and there is no misreading his attitude. This cat is not friendly. He skulks alongside my cage as well, but his grass-colored eyes are not simply curious—they are glaring in at me, studying me, disliking me. This cat rounds his back and pitches his ears back. "Sssssssss," he says. His lips curl back as the hiss slips through his tightly clenched teeth.

"Grrrrr!" I am startled to realize that this quick low growl has come from *me*.

I back up and bury myself as thoroughly as I can in the cloth, clawing into its folds. With a cat on either side of me, I am almost completely surrounded by dark fur; their bodies are nearly as long as my cage, and their haunches alone are larger than all of me—I feel as tiny as one of the lizards my mother used to catch for breakfast, and as helpless. Will the angry cat reach in to swat me? Will he overturn my cage? Will the cat who seems friendly help me?

"Well hello, boys! I see you've found the baby." It is the woman's voice, warbling. The cats turn to look at her as she walks in and sits down next to my cage. "She's been a sick little kitty," the woman says, and the longer cat arches his back upwards to meet her hand as she scratches him near his tail. "Mommy brought her home to try to help her get well," she says, as the all-dark, heavier cat takes his attention totally away from me and walks over to demand petting from her other hand. "You boys need to be nice to her!"

I relax a bit, relieved. With the woman here, the male cats seem to have forgotten me.

"Mmmmmm," purrs the friendly cat.

"Mrrrrrowww," says the heavier cat, demandingly. He reaches his head up toward the woman, opens his mouth and nips her on the nose. She smiles at this sign of affection.

I stare at the woman and the cats as she sits there fondling them. This place where no rain or wind would ever touch you, with its soft places to lie on and its unending supply of food and milk...this place is home to these cats! They are free to wander in it, wherever they please.

And not only that: the woman calls them her boys, and they consider her their mother.

"Darcie! Are you up there?"

There is a man who lives here, too. His voice is deep and booming, bouncing off the walls and rattling me. He acts as if he is the woman's mate, calling to her, nuzzling her, eating with her. He ignores me, not even looking my way, as though unaware that I am locked in here watching him.

The man is standing in the middle of the room where my cage sits. He is hollering toward the open door at the top of the stairs.

"Yes, I'm up here getting ready!" the woman calls down.

"We're supposed to be there in fifteen minutes!"

"Fifteen minutes?" the man says. "I thought it started at seven!"

"No, six!" the woman answers.

The man hurries for the stairs.

Just after daylight brightens the house, a loud laughing voice interrupts the silence, startling me, even though I've heard it before. "Good morning!" it exclaims. "A beautiful morning!" The voice belongs to Tevin, who works here. He drives up in a golf cart whenever the sun is beginning to climb in the sky. Ginger arrives behind him in her own cart. She is the dark woman with the deep Bahamian voice that I remember from when I was wrapped in the warm towels. "Yesss," she says, agreeing with Tevin. And then the hustle-bustle inside the walls of the house begins.

Ginger meanders all over the place, carrying buckets and mops and cloths, cleaning. She often passes my cage as she moves from room to room, but she doesn't speak to me. In fact, she doesn't seem a bit curious about me, not like the other humans who point and poke and ask questions. I wonder at this, because it is Ginger who worked to save my life. Doesn't she care about me now? Maybe she only helped me because the woman who captured me told her to.

Tevin, on the other hand, walks over and studies me when no one else is around. "Hello, pretty little girl," he whispers. I narrow my eyes and stare steadily into his, warning him not to touch me. He returns to the room where the human food is prepared. I hear him in there whistling and making a lot of clatter. Then he calls the humans to the eating room, and he and Ginger carry in the food for them. When Tevin is not cooking or serving food, he works outside. I see him through the glass next to my cage, clipping bushes or picking up the seaweed that washes onto the beach. Sometimes he interrupts his chores to bring a visitor to the door. Humans wander in and out of this place like the chickens and turkeys in the sleeping shed. Some stand and chat, some sit and stay for a while, some even plop down right beside my cage.

"She was probably too fragile to be spayed in the first place," the woman is telling the female human sitting next to her.

"Then why did you do her?" asks the visitor.

"Well, we had the volunteer vet on the island for only one week, and won't have another until next year, so it was now or wait until then. And we didn't realize how weak she was," the woman answers. "But I don't think the surgery was the real problem. On that first night after the operations, we put the cats back into their cages outside of the clinic. We had no idea how cold it was going to get. By the time I got to this little one first thing in the morning, she was lying drenched in a puddle of her own urine, her whole body shaking as though she was having a seizure—she was probably in hypothermia. So I brought her home and we started warming her up right away."

The visitor comes over and sits down next to me. She sticks a finger in between the webbing on the side of my cage and wiggles it. "Here, kitty kitty," she says. "Come over here and let me pet you!"

I think of my mother. If a human had poked a finger toward her, I'm sure she would have bitten it or clawed it. But I feel strangely secure in my small, confined space, and certain that the finger can't get to me. Instead of trying to attack it, I make myself into the tiniest ball of fur possible and scrunch against the back wall of the cage.

"How sad! Did that happen to any of the other cats?" the visitor asks.

"No. After that first night, we learned our lesson and started bringing the cats here to our garage to recover, where they would be warmer."

"I'd love to see her," the visitor says. "She looks awfully pretty."

"I'll take her out for a minute," the woman tells her. "But I don't think she's ready to be touched by strangers yet."

The woman opens the top of the cage and reaches in to pick me up. I fit entirely into the woman's hand, surrounded by her fingers, and feel helplessly small there, and trapped. I am high above the floor—if I could wrestle free and jump down to it, where would I hide? I look around the room, trying to decide. Maybe I could sneak behind the contraption in the corner, or underneath the low-slung table next to the sofa. I look down. The floor is a long way to fall. And then, swish! I am sailing through the air, breeze ruffling through my fur. The woman is moving me, holding me out to the visitor, on display as though I am some sort of prize rat. I flatten myself onto my paws, sinking into the woman's palm.

"Oh, she is pretty," says the visitor. "Look at those gorgeous eyes!" She aims a finger toward me again, and this time I hiss. Just a little hiss; I don't even bare my teeth. It's enough to make her back off.

"Sorry about that," says the woman holding me. "It's really just too soon. She's getting used to a lot of new things."

Sorry? I think. Sorry, even though I didn't show my teeth or make a move toward the visitor? Sorry that I am just trying to keep some space between myself and all these strangers treating me like some kind of lizard they can bat around whenever they want to?

The woman pulls me in tight now, against her chest. She covers me with her hand. Her heart beats against my throat.

"Well, good luck with her," says the visitor. "These wild cats probably just aren't made to be house pets, you know."

"We'll see how it turns out," answers the woman.

When the visitor leaves, the woman sits down by my cage, but doesn't put me in it. Instead, she starts kissing me. My mother used to kiss me with her tongue. It was as rough as the sandpaper discarded by island workers, which we sometimes stumbled upon in our travels. It tickled deliciously, as my mother used it to clean as well as caress me. The woman, though, uses her lips to kiss me, smearing her scent all over my fur, leaving it sticky in spots. The feel of her human mouth is foreign, but disconcertingly soft, like the leisurely flick of a long-haired tail.

"Little Miracle," she whispers again and again as she presses her lips on me, and I feel my body go flaccid like the jellyfish that sometimes wash ashore, a blob of lightly quivering flesh. My paws fall away from my body, my head arches back, my ears rise up to meet her hand.

"*Anybody here?*"

The voice is loud, careening toward us from some faraway spot in the house that I can't see. I hear a distant door creak closed.

"In the living room!" the woman calls back.

It's the man. I tense as his footsteps get closer. And then he sits down, right beside us. The woman strokes me, saying nothing.

The man studies me silently. His eyes travel up and down my body, and I pull in my legs, trying to shield myself. My claws edge out of their sockets. My whiskers stiffen. Finally, he speaks.

"How is her scar coming?" His fingers, thick and sun toughened, reach over to find the stretch of bare skin on my stomach. I cringe as his hand comes toward me, my spine goes rigid as I prepare to resist—but his touch is surprisingly gentle, and I withdraw my claws.

"It looks good, like it's healing well. There are a few stubbles of fur starting to grow back," the woman answers. "She doesn't seem to be in pain from it."

It's true. My full belly strains against the skin, as though the flesh is too snug for my growing body, but I feel fine.

"That's a pretty big snip out of her ear," says the man. "Or maybe it just looks big because she's so tiny."

"Well, she is little, but we also made the notches big, on purpose," the woman answers, lightly fingering my ear.

"Why?" the man asks. "Doesn't anybody who knows about cats recognize the notches?"

"Oh sure," the woman answers. "But we don't want any confusion next time. The notches on the cats that were done that one time years ago are too small. They're hard to see in the traps. We don't want to cart anybody to the clinic who doesn't need to go!"

I wonder who snipped me and why they did it. I don't remember when it was done, but my ear feels no soreness now, only the undeniable pleasure of the woman's finger gently stroking it. The man also reaches over to touch the notch before he walks away, a quick firm grasp that scrunches my ear whiskers, but I do not flinch.

The woman puts me back in the cage, but she doesn't close the door! Instead, she leaves it standing wide open. "You can come out for a few minutes now, little Miracle," she says. "It's time for you to look around and get to know the household. Just come out when you're ready. I'll be sitting right here if you need me."

The woman smiles and walks to a chair across the room, and I am left alone with this invitation to explore. The sudden unexpected freedom frightens me. The house feels too big. It's filled with noises that make me jump: the doors opening and closing, footsteps in other rooms, voices ricocheting off the walls—sounds belonging to humans I can't always see. If I leave my cage, I won't know where to go.

I hunker down beside the box of sand, trying to decide what to do. I look at the stairs. They go a long way up, and I can't see what's beyond the door at the top of them. It's the same with the other door that the man often walks through. When he disappears behind it, I usually hear a squeak and then a settling, as though he is sitting down in a chair, and then I hear hollow clicking sounds, but I don't know what they are.

I study the other doors. I do know what's behind them. Closest to me is the eating room. That door is usually open. From my cage I can see the humans when they sit down in there, using tools to take their food from a table. I can't see behind the other door, but I know it's the kitchen, the room where the food is prepared for the humans. Before their mealtimes, I can smell food odors and hear cooking sounds coming from behind that door.

I listen intently, my ears pointing forward from my head, craning for sounds of any other humans in the house. But I don't perceive any movements or voices. I sniff for the male cats and perk up my ears for their bells, but I don't hear them either.

Cautiously, I creep toward the open door of my cage. I press myself low to the ground, trying to make myself invisible, and stick my nose out. But the woman is watching me, smiling. "That's right, little girl, come on out," she urges. The sound of her voice seems to propel me as I pitch myself forward and onto the sofa, then down to the floor in a clumsy leap. The floor is hard and chilly against my paw pads, and as soon as I hit it, I begin to run toward the eating room.

I lope past the many legs of the chairs in the eating room, toward a short, sand-colored cabinet that is backed up to a wall. I squeeze myself in there, between the back of the cabinet and the wall, where I hope no one can see me, and curl into myself, a silent ball, alert, listening, afraid, unsure of what is expected of me or what I want to do next. How I long for my mother to come and find me, sink her teeth into the nape of my neck and carry me away, back to a mangrove bush or an empty building where we can be together, where my mother can show me what to do.

Instead, it is the woman who finds me. I see her feet first, as I peer out from underneath the cabinet, and then I hear her voice: "Little Miracle, where are you?"

From my hiding place, I watch her feet as they walk into the eating room, and next I see her hands and then her face, as she kneels on the floor and peers between the legs of the chairs, underneath the table. She stands up and I watch her feet begin to walk my way. She halts beside my cabinet, and I hear her fingernails click against its wood. The furniture legs that are nearest me rise up, and the back of the cabinet moves away from the wall. I am exposed.

I tuck my head down tight onto my paws, backing my body against the wall as closely as I can, not looking at the woman but feeling her nearness with my whiskers, as she stoops down and scoops me up into her hand. "Oh, little Miracle, you don't have to hide," she tells me. "You're even shaking, poor thing. Why is that? There's nothing to be afraid of," the woman says, nuzzling my neck.

I take no comfort in her words or her caress. There is much to be frightened of in this enormous, strange space. I am exhausted when she settles me back in my cage and secures the door, shutting me away from any humans who might wander in, and from the male cats who might come by and sniff at me again.

Fingers of shade reach through the window and stretch across my cage when the next visitor arrives. Her face is blotchy, her voice trembles as she walks in with the woman who lives here. She carries a small dark bag, lumpy and knotted closed. She slumps into a chair like a nesting hen sinking onto its breast.

I hop onto the edge of my sand box, trying to see her better, but the edge is too skinny and I lose my balance and fall in the sand. I shake my paws to clean them of debris and try again. This time, I clutch the rim of the box with my claws and stay up long enough to see the visitor's hands draped over the bag. Her fingers twitch. I catch a familiar repulsive whiff and crinkle my nose.

"Where did you find him?" the woman who lives here asks.

"Over by the big yellow house on the bank," the visitor says. "I was out walking, and I saw something dragging itself under a golf cart. I couldn't quite make out what it was, and since nobody was home, I went on up the driveway. By the time I got to the golf cart, he was already dead, poor thing. He'd barely made it underneath."

"I didn't even know we had any cats in that area! How big is he?"

"Oh, no bigger than Miracle. Probably even a little bit smaller. Definitely skinnier."

"What color is he?"

"Orange."

Orange. I turn the word over in my head. I can't picture it.

"Do you want to see him?" the visitor asks.

Yes, I think. Could this be one of my siblings?

"No," the woman answers. "Maybe he comes from one of the calicoes that live by the golf course."

The golf course! My mother never took us there.

"Something has to be done," the visitor says. "Even if we cut down the population, there's not enough food. A kitten this size doesn't even know where to find food!"

Cut down the population? I wonder what she means by that? Will this involve shotguns or poison?

The woman who lives here puts her chin in her hand, staring at the bag. She closes her eyes, sighs, and shakes her head. "Are you sure he died of starvation?" she asks.

"It sure looks like it," answers the visitor.

"Well, I don't know what to do," the woman says. "It's not like we live here all the time and can take food out every night to every corner of the island!"

"I know, I know," says the visitor. "I'm just upset. And I didn't know what to do with him."

"I'll ask Tevin to bury him in the side yard."

"Really? Are you sure you don't mind? I just couldn't stand the thought of throwing him into a trash can or taking him to the incinerator, and there's no place to bury him at the doctor's apartment."

"I understand. Of course we'll bury him."

"Thank you," says the visitor.

"You're welcome, Mandy. Come on, let's go find Tevin."

I strain to hear them as they leave the house, the visitor cradling the bag. I get down and look out the window, trying to see Tevin working on the beach. I can't find him.

I lie beside my bowls and try to sleep.

The next day, the sun has barely broken the sky when the woman creeps softly down the stairs. She comes to my cage but does not speak. She opens its door. She pats the cushion in front of the door as though to say, "Come here!" I back up. She turns and walks toward the kitchen. Her feet are bare. They make the slightest slapping sound against the floor. When I can no longer hear them, I leave my cage. I run to the corner and squeeze myself behind a piece of furniture, listening, sniffing.

I can barely smell the boy cats from back here. Even the human scents are lighter. A gentle gurgle comes from the kitchen, but otherwise the house is silent.

I leave my hiding space and venture down the room, keeping my side plastered to the wall, moving quickly behind a chair and then a little table and then beneath a stack of shelves. I want to peer around the room, decide on an exit to another part of the house and go explore, but the bottom shelf blocks my vision. I put my front feet on it and claw my way up. It's a struggle; there's not a lot of room to maneuver back here. I haul up my hind legs and turn sideways to find my balance, excited by my new view. My tail knocks into something. It falls with a crash to the floor. Small pieces of glass skid across the tile. My fur stands up. I fling myself back down behind the shelves and crouch against the wall. My tail must be longer than I think! And the woman is sure to see my mistake. Will I be in trouble?

The soft slap of feet comes toward me from the kitchen. Then they turn away. I wait, shaking. Should I make a run for it, toward an unknown part of the house? Should I jump back up into my cage?

The feet return. This time they are wearing shoes. The woman squats down by the shelves, spots me against the wall, reaches in for me, grabs me by the nape of the neck and hauls me out. I do not resist. I go limp and stay quiet. I don't know what else to do. Claw her? Bite her? Try to run away?

I think of hurting her. I am sure that my mother would have done anything to get out of this house. I am certain that she would injure any human who tried to hold her. So I imagine sinking my fangs into the woman's hand, then pushing out all my claws and plunging them into the softness of her skin, drawing blood with every puncture. I imagine holding onto her hand as firmly as I can, not letting go as she tries to shake me off. In my scenario, the woman rushes to the door, screaming, opens it, and throws me out. And then I run away to find my mother.

Except that I don't do this. I don't really know where I am. I'm not sure where this house sits on my island. I don't recognize the beach that I see through the window or the stretch of road out front. I always sniff intensely at the quick bursts of air I get when an outside door opens, but it doesn't smell like my territory. I am uncertain that I would ever find my mother again. And I would have to find food on my own.

"It's okay, Miracle," the woman whispers against my head. Her breath is warm and rustles the whiskers just inside my ear. "Everybody has accidents, especially clumsy little kitties getting used to being in a house." She wraps me in her hands, against her chest. She carries me through the kitchen and into a little room. She stops beside a box that sits on the floor, a low, long box that's much bigger than the one filled with sand in my cage. This box holds a kind of dirt I've never seen before. It's not quite sand and not quite gravel, and it sticks to my feet when she sets me down in it. "This is what house kitties use to avoid another kind of accident altogether. Would you like to learn about it?"

The small pebbles smell of the big male cats. It is the un-mistakable odor of their urine and feces. These are the scents of alien cat territory, clearly marked. Even the whiskers on my legs seem to take offense at the dirt as I sit in it—they lift up and away from my fur. Why does the woman plop me right in the middle of this? What does she expect me to do here?

I want to leap out and dash away, but she is kneeling right beside the box. So I hunker down and wait, my stomach tight against my paws, my chin practically touching the pebbles. I remember how my mother would lick the bellies of my siblings and me when we were first born, stimulating our bowels and bladders to open. Now, I tighten them, refusing to emit any waste that will let the other cats know I've invaded their space.

The woman stays there beside the box, looking at me, talk-ing to me in a voice that rolls like the waves, or like the songs of birds: "This is the litter box, little Miracle, where house kitties do their business."

I am not a house kitty. I do nothing.

"Okay, Miracle, maybe we'll try again later," the woman says. She has to dig into the dirt to pick me up, scooping me from beneath my belly, but she doesn't seem to mind. She even nuzzles my head as she carries me back to my cage. But she gives me another bath with the wipes before she locks me in it.

"Fred! Frisco! Good morning!" the woman calls toward the stairs. I hear the male cats' bells clinking against their collar tags as they scamper down to find her. These are their names. They are not simply called "boys." Fred is the dark and light cat who looks like a man wearing a tuxedo, the clothing human males wear on dress-up nights here on the island, nights when there are big parties and we know there will be tasty leftovers in the trash. Frisco is the all-dark one, skittish and leery of everyone except the woman. The woman reaches down to pat the tops of their heads as they rub against her legs. She scratches underneath their collars. They seem at ease with these belts of cloth fastened tightly around their necks, even proud of them. They use their knuckles to clean the fur around the shiny tags that hang from underneath their chins. They shake their heads for no apparent reason other than to hear the bells clinking against the thin metal tags, making a light tinny music that reverberates off the high ceilings.

"Come on," the woman says, leading the boys away. "Mommy will get your breakfast ready." They follow close on her heels.

The woman always calls herself "Mommy" when she's talking to Fred or Frisco—or me. But other people call her Darcie. That's what the man calls her. "Darcie, do you know where I left my glasses?" he will ask. Or, "Darcie, do you have to spend a lot of time in the office today?" Or, "Hey Darcie, do you want to go for a dive this afternoon?"

"I saw them on the kitchen counter this morning," she will answer. Or, "A couple of hours ought to do it." Or, "Yes, that would be fun—the water is nice and flat." The woman calls the man Ray.

Everyone in this human house has a name. Even me. And mine is about to get longer.

I've eaten, slept, stretched, endured a visit from the boy cats and am feeling restless when the man who lives here walks in and up the stairs. The stairs are painted metal and ascend in a semi-circle. The dull clang of shoe against metal resounds with each step, on rungs that rise and swirl taller than a coconut palm. At the top of the stairs is a landing. The man called Ray walks across the landing and into the room beyond it. I can no longer see him, but I can hear his voice talking to the woman called Darcie.

"I've been thinking. Should we name the kitten?" he asks tentatively. "I mean, it looks like she's becoming a member of the household. Seems like she should have a name."

They are talking about me. My muscles tense. My ears stand up.

"That is a lovely thought!" the woman says. "But I believe I've named her already. Haven't you noticed that I've been calling her Miracle?" I think I hear a smile in her voice. "It seemed like an appropriate name, just because she survived. It's a bit of a miracle, you know?"

"Oh," the man says, and in his voice I think I hear something that sounds oddly like relief, as though he had been wondering whether she would scold him or laugh at him for thinking about naming me. He plunges ahead. "I was thinking that she looks like a Lucy."

"How'd you come up with that?" the woman asks.

"I don't know...she just looks like a Lucy."

"Oh, the way Fred looked like a Fred when you picked him out at the shelter?" the woman asks, half teasing and half mocking.

"Something like that," the man answers.

The woman does not answer. There is silence.

Thump thump.

I hear my heartbeat.

Th-thump. Th-thump.

Something important is being decided: *my* future! They are contemplating giving me a name approved by both of them, declaring me an accepted member of the household. Does this mean that I will never be let out of this house? Does it mean that I will spend most of my life in a cage? If so, I don't want this name! Still, I am anxious about the silence from upstairs. What happens if they decide *not* to name me? And what does a Lucy look like?

At last, the woman answers. "All right then, we'll call her Lucy Miracle," she says. "It's a pretty big name for such a little cat, but it's pretty!" I hear footsteps and rustling. The man and the woman, I suppose, nuzzling again.

I think that what I have just heard is the sound of myself officially being adopted.

Adopted…that probably means that I can have all the food I want forever, just like Fred and Frisco. Maybe the humans expect me to grow up to look like Fred and Frisco, sturdy and strong. Maybe it even means that the humans *like* me as much as they like their boy cats. Maybe they expect me to become part of their family and to remain in this house for always, so that I will never have to hunt for shelter or food.

What makes them think I'd even *want* to be adopted? I am an island cat! We are born free, out in the open air, able to go where we want, when we want. Yes, there are dangers, but my mother taught me about them—I don't need to depend on the protection of fickle humans, here in their closed, air-conditioned house. I miss the scent of the sea air! I want to gallop along the beach, kicking up sand, the salt spray tickling my nose. I want to feel the breeze in my fur again, and fall asleep to the gentle sound of the waves lapping against the shore. I want to roam, and practice my hunting, and grow up to take care of myself. So what if I never feel the caress of the woman's hands again, the deliciousness of those wipes against my belly—I will find my mother to snuggle against!

Do the humans even think about my mother, I wonder?

Does it matter to them that she is still out there on our island somewhere, searching for me? Do they care that I miss her? Do they have any idea of my mother's courage, or the resilience of the island cats, surviving through generations of torment and killing? Or do the humans think that just because they have power over me—the power to cage me, the power to pick me up in their hands, even the power to make me purr when they feed and bathe and pet me—that my mother doesn't matter, that I don't care whether I ever run with my relatives again?

Or could the humans think that this is what my mother would *want* for me? Do they know that my mother spent most of her time teaching us how to find food and showing us that the best food comes from humans? Would they think our constant hunger means that cats must want their own humans?

I remember how exhausted my mother was from all her hunting and relocating, and how relieved when my siblings were strong enough to go off on their own and take care of themselves. But she knew she'd see them often, traveling the territory we all shared. If the humans don't let me go, she and I might never see each other again. I will have to get away from here—adopted or not—if I am ever to see my *real* family again. Who do these humans think they are, to decide my fate without even considering what I might want?

"I wish I had a pink one, but this will have to do," the woman is saying. "I can get her a girlie one when we go home."

"Yes, she deserves a little bit of bling," the man says. "She's pretty enough."

The woman holds me on her lap, firmly—or rather, somewhere near her lap. She is gripping me between her knees, her bones settled in against my rib cage so that I cannot move. She pulls a collar over my nose, around my ears, and onto my neck. The collar is speckled in shades that are meant to resemble cat fur, I think—although it doesn't match my fur at all. At the back of my neck, I feel the snap of the collar being fastened.

"Oh, and it's way too big for her, too!" the woman says. The collar flops loosely around my throat. The woman wrestles with it a while, trying to tighten it. The sensation of human hands around my neck is nerve-wracking. The man called Ray is watching from the chair next to us.

"I'll go get some tape," he says. He comes back with a strip of something clear and sticky, and they use that to tack up the extra length of collar. Now the collar is no longer flopping, but it feels thick and bunched up beneath my chin.

I practice absolute submission during this process, paws tucked beneath my belly, as still and silent as I can be. I clench my teeth to hold in my anger, restrain myself from snarling. I know that I am much too small to get away; their hands would overwhelm me before I could run. My teeth and claws would be no match against all of those hands and fingers. And even if I did escape, I could run only back to my cage, or maybe behind the sofa, before those hands would come and seize me once again. So, like a grasshopper cornered and helpless before the jaws of a cat, I surrender, quaking lightly.

"That's about as good as it gets for now," the man says, poking a finger between the collar and my fur. "I think that's just about the right size, not too tight."

"Okay, thanks for the help," the woman says, carrying me back to my cage. I guess being a full-fledged member of the household, named and collared, does not mean that I get to roam around completely free like the boys do.

Inside the cage, I shake my head, testing the collar. It itches but does not loosen, and the bell jingles harshly in my ear. And then, I hear the jangle of another bell, moving quickly across the landing, down the stairs, into my room and onto my sofa. It's Frisco, hindquarters up, ears forward, whiskers alert,

lips back, eyes wide, staring at me. Of course! The other part
of being collared! The humans and cats can always hear where
you are. I've gotten accustomed to keeping track of the boys by
listening for their bells. Now they will be able to do the same
with me. Except that I'm usually not very hard to keep track
of, cooped up here in my prison like one of the island roosters
when the humans decide there are too many of them and set
out traps for a roundup.

I hiss at Frisco, a long, low hiss that starts deep in my
throat and travels all the way onto his whiskers. Frisco's eyes
blink as he backs up a couple of leg lengths. He raises his head
and slinks slowly away from me, then jumps off the sofa and
ambles casually back up the stairs.

Alone, I try to comfort myself. My new human name and
the collar mean that I have a home here, with its shelter and
food. And yet they almost certainly mean that I will never
again be free to wander the island, to roll in the grass, to feel
the direct heat of the sun on my back, not filtered through a
window. I will never again get to swish my tail along the ground
as I watch the birds overhead in the trees. I will never chase a
lizard among the ferns. Worst of all, I will never be free to find
my mother. I don't want to betray her and my siblings—or any
of the island cats—by becoming a contented, overfed housecat.
I belong out there, on the island, with them. I rock side to
side, from elbow to elbow, agitated, unable to nap.

I am a captive, yet as the days go by, my uneasiness
lessens. There is a predictable routine here, a rhythm to life
in the house that is somehow comforting.

I learn that the room at the top of the stairs is a sleeping
room. When the sky is dark and the stars are high, the man
and the male cats disappear into that room, and usually stay
there until after sunrise. The woman does too, but since I was

collared, she is the last to climb the stairs. She stops by my cage before going up and opens my door, leaving it ajar in the dark. "Goodnight, Lucy Miracle," she whispers quietly. "I'll see you in the morning." Then she retires, and I am free to wander the house, without even the woman watching me.

I wait until it is completely quiet, except for the sounds of slumber: the occasional snore from the sleeping room, the light jingle of one of the other cats' bells as he scratches himself, the rustle of someone turning over. Then I creep out of my cage, as silently as I can in the midnight, not wanting to jangle my own bell, and I wander the many rooms, exploring.

There is a feeding area for the male cats in the room where I was first conscious and wrapped in warm towels. On a low bench against the wall sits a bowl of food for each of them and a deep dish of water. The bench smells of Fred and Frisco's whiskers and saliva. But in the night I don't let that deter me.

I back up several leg lengths, then pump my paws forward and leap toward the bench. I miss and fall into a heap on the floor, skidding backwards across the tile. The rattle of my bell is as loud as a thunderclap. Surely it has traveled up the stairs and woken the others. I lower my body closer to the floor and perk up my ears. If I hear any movement upstairs, I am prepared to run back to my cage or to a closer hiding place.

But all is quiet upstairs. I pick myself up and decide to try a new tactic. I stand beside the bench and hurl myself straight up, front legs stretched as far as they will go. I grip the bench at the edge, where the wood curls downward and tapers off. I pull my back paws toward my belly and heave myself upward. As I lug my stomach onto the bench, I knock the deep bowl, sloshing water everywhere, including my face and front paws. If the water bowl had not been filled all the way up to the brim, perhaps I would not have spilled it. The food bowls are half full. I lick myself dry and help myself to the food; it seems safe while the males are upstairs sleeping. Then I lounge beside the bowls for a while, cleaning my paws and mouth, and mingling my smells with theirs.

I tiptoe down the hall and sniff at the box that holds the waste from the male cats, then head for the sofa in the television room. It is covered with a bulky, soft blanket and is clearly a favorite lounging spot for Fred and Frisco; strands of their dark hairs intertwine with the raveled threads. I knead the blanket as I used to knead my mother's chest, trying to draw milk. It comforts me, smelling as it does of feline contentment. I fall asleep here, awakening with the sunrise, or to the sound of human footsteps or cat bells, when off I run to one of my hiding places.

When the sun is high enough to be seen over the rocks in the ocean, the woman finds me and clutches me to her. Another day begins. I am locked in my cage on the sofa. I eat. I drink. I despair. I watch Fred and Frisco, free to go outside onto a patio just beyond my window. They can travel back and forth, in and out, out and in, through a tiny opening in the wall that is left propped open just for them.

Fred is much more adventurous than Frisco, coming and going frequently. I hear his bell bounce with him across the floor, then fade into the distance as he scampers out. Through my window I see him on the patio, lounging on the warm bricks or scratching on the trees, idly chasing a bug or a leaf in the breeze. Some of his behaviors mystify me. A bananaquit or a swallow—even a huge, bright-breasted robin—can land on the patio, practically in his face, and Fred doesn't chase it. He simply flicks his tail, staring at the bird, not even twitching his whiskers. A tall bougainvillea hedge—so dense that sunlight can barely break through it—surrounds the patio. Fred never tries to climb it, undoubtedly deterred by the long, wicked briars of the bougainvillea. Nor does he try to dig an escape route under it. He seems perfectly content to amuse himself within its confines.

Frisco likes to visit the patio as soon as he and Fred are allowed out after sleeping. He noses around and meows, announcing the new scents that have arrived overnight: dirt left behind by a hermit crab dragging itself across the stones, bird droppings, a dead insect. But when Tevin booms, "Good morning," Frisco darts out of sight, and soon I hear the jingle of his bell in the sleeping room. He spends most of his day up there, away from the noise and activity of the household.

When he does venture downstairs, Frisco ignores me. But Fred stops by often to sniff at me, and he is decidedly friendly. I can tell by his eyes and the way his ears stand up, alert and curious, that he is trying to figure out who I am and means me no harm. Occasionally he offers a curious "Meow?" inviting me to respond. But I don't. I never encourage his visits, sitting motionless in the back of my cage until he leaves. He doesn't stay long.

Both the woman and the man come by often, opening my cage from the top, reaching in to hoist me out and cuddle me for a while. The woman grabs me by the nape of my neck when she picks me up, just as my mother used to do. She coos at me, clasping me tightly against her chest, where I can hear her heartbeat. "Little Lucy Miracle," she sings, kissing the top of my head, my ears, and the back of my neck. My purring surprises me, the vibration of it catching me off guard.

The man usually takes hold of me from underneath, putting his hand under my stomach and raising me up and out of the cage like a shell off the beach. The first few times, I am scared because the man's hands are so much bigger than the woman's. But his hands never hurt me, and there is that baffling, strange sensation of feeling protected by them. He scratches my ears, more roughly than the woman. But far from irritating me, it feels good, like rubbing up against the ragged bark of a tree.

On a quiet morning when the sun is climbing the sky and I am snoozing, both the man and the woman walk in, talking. Neither one comes to my cage. Instead, they sit down in the chairs in front of me. Their voices are edgy, and the fur on my back stands up a bit as I grow nervous.

"I don't want to. She's too little," says the woman.

"But we have to," says the man. "We're going home tomorrow. We certainly can't take her to Florida with us; she doesn't have papers to enter the states. And besides, two cats are enough."

"Tevin and Ginger could take care of her here, until we get back and until she gets bigger," the woman answers. "Then we could let *her* decide."

"She'll decide now," says the man, sure of himself.

"No she won't. She'll just be scared," the woman argues. "She won't know what to do, she won't know where she is."

"Do you want to return her to her territory?" asks the man.

"No—this house has probably become her territory by now. If we took her all the way down there to fend for herself and she couldn't, she'd never be able to find her way back here."

"Look," says the man, growing testy, "she's a feral cat. She might not want to be locked up inside. We owe it to her to give her a choice. That's all I'm saying."

"I understand that," says the woman, "but she's such a baby. She's still frightened. She just lost her mother and she's still getting used to everything around her: us, the house, the boys. Even the patio would probably be too strange and scary. It's not the right time for her to make a choice. She wouldn't even know how to feed herself, all alone on the island."

"Here's what we'll do," argues the man. "We'll walk outside

with her and put her down, just for a minute. If she stays with us, we'll know that's what she wants. If she doesn't, that's her choice."

The woman sits silently, looking down at her hands.

I catch myself panting. They are thinking of setting me free, of putting me back outside on my island, where I will be able to ramble in the open air and search for my mother! I will have to hunt, too, but my belly is so full that it will likely carry me far. Maybe I will even find my mother before I am hungry again. Will the woman agree to let me go? I watch her anxiously.

After many breaths, she looks up from her hands and rises. She opens the cage and grasps me by the neck, as gently as ever. She holds me close, kissing me. I am shaking. "Okay," she says to the man. "You win. We'll try it."

He stands up, walks over to a door at the far end of the living room, and opens it. I smell the palm trees, the sand, the beach, the outdoor odors floating toward me on the brisk ocean breeze, laced with salt. It is the smell of freedom and fear, intermingled, inextricable. The woman gives me one last kiss, harder than usual, in the middle of my skull, her lips lingering on my fur. "I love you, Lucy Miracle," she whispers with a catch in her voice, and then she steps through the door to the island waiting outside and puts me down on the grass.

I hesitate, quivering. I hear myself cry, a piercing, long, uncertain, throaty wail. And then, as though powered by some force deep inside, a force I barely recognize, I run. It is not a choice; it is compulsion. I run to a bougainvillea bush and huddle against it, barely feeling its stickers, still crying. The woman and the man step toward me. I turn, frantically surveying the foreign territory.

And then once again, I run. Faster this time, from grass to the shade of coconut trees to sand. I am shocked by the sudden openness of the beach, the brilliant glare of its expanse in the midday sunlight. I am away from the humans now, and I pause in a small patch of turtle grass that has washed up and dried on the shore. I blink, study the sway of the coastline. I do not recognize it. I open my mouth and turn my head to inhale the smells surrounding me. There is a trace of cats, but none of their odors are familiar. I can see houses, but none that I know. I must indeed be far from my territory. Where should I go?

The wind is picking up. I need shelter, a place to rest and hide, a chance to think. I spy a small building with an open door just beyond a stand of trees and gallop toward it, plowing through the sand. Inside the door is a warm room, dimly lit by a small window. Along a wall sit big shiny machines, shaped like boxes. The closest one has a window in it, through which I see crumpled human clothing. I slither along the space between the machines and the wall, a space barely big enough for me to move through. I duck into the soft wads of lint there, digging into them until I am almost covered. As I grow still, my bell ceases its jingling. Eventually, my heart begins to slow and exhaustion overcomes my fear. By the time the thunder and lightning begin, I am falling asleep.

I wake up at the sound of human voices. The room has darkened with the sky outside, and the storm has given way to a gentle rain, lapping against the window. I open my eyes and lift my head, groggily trying to remember where I am. I turn my ear to the sound of the voices coming from just outside the door. I recognize one of them. It belongs to the man called Ray.

"What's this door, Viktor?"

Another male voice, jagged and quick, answers. "The laundry room," it says, and then feet are inside the door, and a hand flips the switch that makes human houses light up.

In the sudden brightness I am wide-awake. A drainpipe twists and curls over my head, tight to the wall. Maybe I can squeeze myself in there. I hunker down, ready myself, and leap toward the pipe. My claws slip off the metal, and I plummet back to the lint pile. My bell jingles as I fall.

"Ssh! I think I hear her!" says Ray, excitedly.

"I heard it too," Viktor agrees. "She is behind the dryer."

Feet charge toward my hiding place, one set flopping loudly in sandals, the other set clomping in boots. I cower in the lint as the dryer whooshes away from the wall and the men dash around it to stare down at me.

Ray scoops me up. "Thanks a lot, Viktor," he says.

"No problem," Viktor answers, pushing the dryer back against the wall. And then we are walking out of the laundry room and across the sand and over the grass and onto the sidewalk and in through the door that leads to the room with my sofa, and there sits the woman, crying by my cage, hands wiping her wet cheeks. She is talking to Ginger, who is standing next to her.

"I knew we shouldn't have let her out. I shouldn't have agreed. She must be terribly frightened. The thunder and lightning would be so scary to a little cat like that. She wouldn't know what to do, all alone in the rain like this," the woman called Darcie is saying. Ginger nods and grunts. Then she sees me crossing the room in Ray's hands, and her teeth sparkle in her smooth face. It is the biggest smile I have ever seen from Ginger.

"Look!" Ginger says, tapping the woman's shoulder to interrupt her crying. Ray holds me out to the woman called Darcie, as she leaps up with disbelief in her eyes. She takes me from the man. First she kisses him, and then she kisses me, and then they are both crying. I do not struggle or speak. I am struck dumb by the question that darts through my head: am I back where I belong?

Another sunrise, and the woman carries me to the litter box again. This time Tevin comes with her. "Bring her in here several times a day," the woman tells him, setting me down in the box, "and do this to help her get the idea." The woman uses her fingers to claw at the pebbly dirt, digging a hole. Then she sits me on it. I go limp, as I always do. I have no intention of leaving my products in the male cats' territory.

"Oh, okay," says Tevin, squatting down beside the box and watching. "I see how you do it."

"If you keep it up—just teaching her to dig in the litter, a few times every day—sooner or later she'll catch on," the woman continues.

To me, she says, "Do your business, Lucy," and waits while I sit scrunched in the box, unwilling to use it and unable to escape. "Okay then, maybe next time little girl," she says, and picks me up. Tevin walks with her back to the living room and my cage, and she gives him instructions all along the way.

"Now remember to feed her first thing when you get here in the morning, and again before you leave at night," she says. "Make sure her water bowl is full. Change the towels on the bottom of her cage, and keep them clean. Talk to her a lot. Say her name. Just say it over and over: Lucy, Lucy, Lucy Miracle. That way she'll get to know that it's her name."

"Yes, okay," Tevin says, nodding his head at each command.

"Ginger!" calls the woman.

"Yes?" answers Ginger, walking slowly into the room.

"You don't have to touch Lucy while we're gone," says the woman. "I know that you are still not that comfortable with cats—such a loss for you!" she says with a tease to her voice, kissing me on the head. "But you do need to help Tevin feed her and keep her cage clean. Okay?"

Although Ginger looks as apprehensive as I feel, she agrees. "Okay," she says, "but if I reach in her cage, she might scratch me."

"No, she won't," says the woman, with a little chuckle at the thought. "She's just a tiny thing who's never scratched anyone, and she's glad to get her food and water. She won't hurt you!"

"Okay, then," says Ginger, distrustfully, in her gravelly Bahamian voice.

Then the woman called Darcie kisses me one more time, a lingering kiss reminiscent of the one before she put me outside. "We have to go home to Florida for a while. We'll be back before you know it, little Lucy Miracle," she says. "Tevin and Ginger will take good care of you and we'll see you when we get back."

"Hey Dar! Ready for the round-up?" the man called Ray yells from upstairs.

"Yes, I guess so," the woman answers. She puts me inside my cage and latches the door. "And don't forget to let her out to wander around and learn the house," she adds to Tevin and Ginger. "She might feel more comfortable about it while the boys aren't here, so let her out a lot."

"Okay," answers Tevin once again, nodding yes, yes. "I will do it."

"I've got the big boy, if you can get the baby," Ray calls down from over the railing that leads to their sleeping room.

"Okay. I think I know where he is," answers the woman. She heads toward the other end of the house as Ray walks down from their room, Fred in his arms. The woman returns in a couple of minutes carrying Frisco, and they put both cats into a carrier and close it up. The males settle down docilely, their grassy eyes shining out from behind the screening on the side of the carrier. Ray picks them up and walks toward the door that leads to the garage.

"Bye, Lucy Miracle," the man and the woman both call to me. "We'll be back."

I hear the squeal of golf carts backing up as they leave, off to Florida, wherever that is.

Later, when the sun is high, Tevin and Ginger are angry at each other, and it's about me.

I ventured out of my cage earlier to relieve myself, and two little products of my movement sit on the sofa. I prefer to leave them on the sofa, rather than in the small box of sand in my cage, which is so close to my sleeping and sitting area—and to my food. Whenever the woman called Darcie would see this, she would get a paper towel and pick up my leavings, then spray something that smells a little like trees onto the sofa and scrub it. After that, she would carry me once again to the male cats' box and tell me, "*This* is where house kitties do their business, Lucy Miracle."

Ginger, however, apparently doesn't want to touch my leavings any more than she wants to touch me. "I am not going to clean up poop!" she protests to Tevin.

"But Gin," Tevin says, his voice even louder than usual, "we have to clean it up. We have to take care of the little girl until Ray and Darcie get back!"

"Well then, YOU clean it up!" says Ginger, stomping off toward the kitchen.

"Woman!" yells Tevin. "Let me show you how easy this is!" He returns with a paper towel and the sprayer, and cleans up my mess as Ginger watches, arms crossed over her chest. "See that?" Tevin says to Ginger. "How hard is that? See," holding out his hands to her, "my hands didn't even get dirty."

"I don't care," growls Ginger, stubbornly. "I am not going to clean cat poop."

"But you are the housekeeper!" yells Tevin. "It is your job."

"My job is not to clean poop!" Ginger answers obstinately.

"Oh, Gin, you are too spoiled!" Tevin tells her. "A little dirty work do you good!"

Ginger stomps off to the kitchen again, and I slink to the back of my cage as Tevin goes to the garage, mumbling all the way. "Spoiled woman," I think he is saying. From the kitchen, I hear a cabinet door slam.

Now, after every sunrise, when Tevin and Ginger arrive, they argue about who will clean up my messes. Tevin has carried me to the male cats' box a few times, but I am terrified, shaking and limp until it's over, and he puts me back in my cage. After a while, he gives up and leaves me alone.

When Tevin and Ginger are here, I spend the time cringing on my towel, eating, and trying to sleep. Lots of frightening noises punctuate the daylight in this house: beeping from the kitchen, angry sucking sounds from the vacuum that Ginger hauls around, swirling water from the bathrooms, pots banging as Tevin makes lunch and cleans the kitchen, the loud jangle of the telephone on the table beside my sofa, doors slamming with people coming and going, talking, laughing, arguing. Tevin talks even more loudly than usual with the family gone. He visits and laughs with other island workers who are his friends, or with the residents who come by to borrow a tool or some provisions from the kitchen.

"What is *that*?" a woman asks as she lets the door slam shut behind her. She stops short and crinkles her nose as though she has smelled something rotten.

"What's what?" Tevin asks, emerging from the kitchen.

"*That!*" the woman answers, pointing at me. "In the cage."

"That's a cat," Tevin tells her.

"No way Gin is keeping a cat!" the woman says, shaking her head.

"It's not her cat, it's Darcie and Ray's. GIN!" Tevin yells, setting my fur on edge. I feel it rise along the ridge of my back.

Ginger walks in, wiping her hands on a towel. "Hey, Petunia!" she says.

Petunia doesn't offer any human niceties like hello. "Whatchyou doin' with a cat?" she asks. Her voice is almost as loud as Tevin's and nearly as deep.

"Darr-say caught her during TNR," Ginger says.

"TNR?" Petunia asks, still staring at me. "What is TNR?"

"Trap, neuter, release," Tevin jumps in, authoritatively. "They do it in the states."

"No," Ginger says. "That's not the real name. It's trap, neuter...trap, neuter..." Ginger stops to think. The hand not holding the towel reaches up to twist her earring. Her eyes look toward the ceiling. "*Return!*" she announces triumphantly. "Trap, neuter, *return*."

"I never heard of no trap neuter anything," says Petunia. "Why you want to trap cats?"

"Darr-say and her friends want to fix them so they can't make babies," Ginger tells her. "So there'll be fewer cats on the cay."

"So why you have one in your living room?" asks Petunia.

"This one was sick," Ginger says. "So she didn't get returned to where she come from. We kept her here, treated her like a baby. Now Darr-say doesn't want to let her go. Tevin and I are supposed to take care of her."

"Hmmph!" grunts Petunia. "I never thought I'd live to see the day that Gin would be takin' care of a cat livin' inside a house on a couch!" The women giggle, the sounds bubbling up from deep in their throats.

Trap, neuter, return. That's what happened to me—all but the return part. The woman called Darcie said "no" when her mate asked whether she wanted to return me to my territory, but maybe my mother was returned to where we came from. Does she search for me there?

A pain swells in my chest as Ginger and Petunia head back to the kitchen and Tevin walks outdoors. I recognize it. It is the pain of loneliness.

The humans talk about me and feed me, but no one comes to cuddle me now; no one is nice to me in the way that the woman called Darcie was. There are no moments of pleasure, being bathed and held. I spend my days agitated and anxious: freedom lies just beyond my window, or through the crack of a door, and yet I cannot escape. I am lonely, but I do not want the humans to touch me. I do not know when the family will return or what will become of me.

One day when the sun is blazing, I am lying on the sofa watching Tevin trim palm trees along the beach. He climbs a tall ladder up into a tree, carrying a machete. Its razor-sharp edge glints in the sun. Tevin hoists the machete and whacks at the branches with brisk, angry chops. The palm fronds tumble to the ground. From time to time, a coconut falls and bounces once in the sand.

Inside, Ginger clambers down the stairs, hauling her water bucket and mopping each step behind her as she goes. When she reaches the bottom of the stairs, she wrings the mop and puts it in the bucket. But instead of picking up the bucket and walking out of the room without looking at me—as she usually does—she stops, hands on her hips, and turns toward me. Our eyes hold on to each other. As Ginger stares at me and says nothing, I become nervous. I break my gaze, scamper into my cage, and mash myself back into a corner.

Ginger begins to walk toward me, slowly. I hold my breath, afraid that she is coming for me. It can't be to pet me or to take me out, because Ginger never does those things. I remember the woman called Darcie assuring Ginger that I wouldn't scratch her, but I make plans to do just that if Ginger dares to stick her hand in my cage. With Tevin on the beach, I am totally alone—even if I were to screech or meow for help, he wouldn't hear me. I will have to scratch her to scare her away.

But Ginger stops just before the sofa and sinks down into a chair. I have never seen Ginger sit before. She clasps her hands in her lap and looks at me for many long breaths. Her face seems to soften. Puzzled, I lower my eyelids and look downward, signaling that I don't want any kind of confrontation. Then Ginger speaks. What she says is only one word, but it startles me into opening my eyes, lifting my ears, and looking at her fixedly once again.

"Luu-cy," Ginger says, in her guttural voice. Her tone is not unfriendly, but she doesn't seem to be calling me, and clearly she is not starting a conversation. It's almost as though she is trying out my name.

I gape, perplexed, as Ginger says it once more: "Lucy." Then she unclasps her hands, gets out of the chair, picks up her mop and bucket, and leaves the room, never looking at me again. Confused and spent, I watch her go. And then I flee in the only way I can: into the comfort of sleep.

The woman called Darcie said she would be back, but moon after moon rises and falls from the sky, and she does not return. I think of the times that my mother and I watched a human female feeding a cat that came each day to her garage. The woman would pour crispy food into a dish on the cement floor and the cat would eat his fill. Then he would jump onto the seat of a golf cart parked in the garage and snooze contentedly. My mother and I would sometimes sneak into the garage while he slept and gobble any leftovers from the bowl. How we envied that cat! Plump, contented, unharmed by the human who fed but never touched him.

Then came the day when we wandered by and the garage door was closed, the windows were shuttered, and the cat lay outside the house, hungry. He stayed there for days, growing thinner and thinner. Dependent on a fickle human, he had forgotten his hunting skills. I am fearful of becoming a cat like him.

I sleep as much as possible during sunlight, waiting for the solitude of the nights. When the dark settles in, the house is hushed, and I am alone. I prowl the rooms, looking for an escape, but every door and window is shut tight. Even the opening in the wall for the boys is bolted closed. I detect the faintest scent of the outside air through one rotting board in a door that leads to the beach yard. I work at it with my claws, scratching, scratching, but I cannot break through.

From the window near my sofa, I see other cats freely walking back and forth across the yard. Sometimes alone, sometimes in pairs, they are protected by the darkness. I launch myself onto a small, glass-topped table beside the sofa to get a better view of the outdoors, but my claws can't hold on, and I skid across the glass, crashing into the base of a lamp. The lamp teeters but doesn't fall. Why do humans put so many obstacles in their living spaces? I stand up, shake myself off, walk carefully around the lamp and press my nose to the glass. I can see much further out onto the yard and beach from here. The next time a cat walks by, I scrape the glass with my claws, using both paws. He doesn't even glance my way.

I think about my mother during these long nights, wishing for the solace of her body to snuggle against, wondering whether she is lonely for me. I imagine her foraging for food, consumed by her daily struggle to survive. I suspect that I am at the farthest end of the island, and I have little hope of seeing her; she would not travel this distance. Occasionally, though, I see a cat with the same sand and dirt markings as my mother and me, and a pang of longing stabs my gut—sharp, like the needle that punctured us that night when I last saw her.

When I am finally exhausted, I fall asleep, until the rising sun wakes me and my uneasy life resumes.

The tone of Tevin and Ginger's conversation has changed.

"I must tell you something," I hear Ginger say loudly from the kitchen, and then she closes the door leading into the room where my cage sits.

I move to the side of my cage closest to the kitchen and lift my ears as tall as they will go, pushing them forward and straining to hear—but from behind the door, I catch only occasional words and phrases. Some of the words make my fur stand on end. "Traps…" I hear Ginger say. And "…doesn't like cats…" And "…catch them."

Tevin's voice is louder, and I can hear him ask Ginger questions. "Why?" and "When?" he asks.

And then a word from Ginger that recalls the horrors I have heard. "Poison," Ginger utters.

I struggle to make some sense of what I am hearing. Are they planning to trap and poison cats? No, they wouldn't do that! Not Tevin and Ginger! Why, they even feed the turkeys that come to the window every morning, clucking for their breakfast. I've seen both of them crumble bread in their hands and throw it to the turkeys, or dish up the birdseed mixed with corn that's kept in a big container especially for them. Could it be that someone else is poisoning cats on the island? Is my mother safe? Or are Tevin and Ginger talking about me? Are they going to poison me while Darcie is away, tired of having to feed me, tired of my messes?

I get no more clues, because Tevin ends the conversation. "We must tell Darcie," he commands. Relief. It can't be me they are going to poison. The door to my room opens. Tevin and Ginger walk toward me. I creep to the back of my cage, crumple down onto my paws.

"They are coming tomorrow," Ginger is saying to Tevin. "I need to clean extra—it stinks in here. And look at those paw prints on the table. She should not be allowed on the table. I cannot keep the glass clean with her here."

"So clean extra," says Tevin. "Polish the glass." His voice is sharper now than it was when I heard it coming from the kitchen.

"Not with the cat in here," Ginger tells him. "Take her outside, so I can scrub everything and she cannot mess it up again."

"I can't take her outside, woman!" Tevin says impatiently to Ginger. "Darcie will kill me if she runs away!"

"Take her outside in her cage," Ginger instructs, equally impatient.

"No, no, she is not going outside!" Tevin retorts, done with the idea.

"Then take her to the garage," Ginger orders him.

"What if she runs away from there?" Tevin asks, his voice growing strident, as it always does during their tussles.

"Keep the doors shut," Ginger answers back. She doesn't shout; Ginger's voice simply gets deeper, slower, more determined. There is a stubborn edge to it that won't be shaken. "That way she can't get out."

"I cannot keep the doors shut! I have to use the lawn mower, and I need the tools! I go in and out of the garage all day!"

"Then put her in the bathroom," Ginger answers, with finality.

"Oh, woman!" Tevin says in disgust, almost hissing. He comes to my cage and grabs it by the handle on top, hoisting it up. I pitch onto my side. "All right, I will put her in the bathroom. You happy now?"

"Remember to give her food and water out there," Ginger tells him.

Tevin stalks out, swinging me like a wattle on a turkey's neck. The door makes its familiar, high-pitched whine as it closes behind us, and Tevin carries me across the garage to a tiny, tiled room. He sets my cage down on the cold, milk-colored floor. "Wait there, girl," he says to me.

I have no choice but to wait—my cage door is closed. I think of Ginger's anxious words: "They are coming tomorrow." Could she be speaking of someone with traps, maybe even poison? Or does she mean the woman called Darcie and her mate, Ray? Are they coming back to me? My skin shivers as I remember the embrace of their hands, the delicious dampness of the baby wipes. I think of the way the woman talks to me as she brings me my food, or pets me, or returns me to my cage. Her voice sings in my head: "Little Lucy Miracle," it says, over and over.

The door to the room opens. It is Tevin, returning with fresh food and water. He puts the bowls in my cage, and when he leaves, he lets my cage door stand open, closing the room's big wooden door behind him. I do not touch the food—or the water.

I crawl out and check my new environment. I am in a room that's no bigger than a clump of trees; it is slick, shiny, with fixtures that rise from the floor. They are the color of coconut meat. The room is smelly of humans and Ginger's cleaning supplies. But there is also a waft of something warm and delicious: the scent of the outdoors...island air! My whiskers tilt upward; my nose twitches; my mouth opens to taste the smell. It is the smell of my home, the scent of grass, palm trees and seawater—the aromas of freedom. My eyes search excitedly for the source of the lovely odor, and there it is above me: a window! Not shut tight with glass, but open, with just a piece of thin wire webbing between the outside and me.

I hop excitedly from the floor to the toilet to the windowsill, and begin to tear frantically at the screen. My claws are tiny, though, against the tight weave of the wire, and it is slow going. Shiny thread by shiny thread, I work at unraveling it, until the outside sheaths of my claws litter the windowsill, and my paws are tired. Then I sleep. Throughout the daylight, I work like this: claw and claw, then nap in exhaustion. Awaken and toil until my claws begin to dull, take another nap. I hear footsteps outside the bathroom door, Tevin coming and going, and I am fearful that he will come inside and catch me at my labor, but all day long, he never opens the door.

By sundown, I have opened up a tiny hole, almost big enough to poke my head through. Another nap, and then I work by the light of the moon, clawing and clawing. My front claws are worn down almost to my paw pads, and they ache.

"Cock a doodle doo!"

"A doodle dooooo!"

The roosters have just begun to crow when I finally manage to cram my head through the screen. The jagged ends of wire claw at my throat, my ears, and my neck as I work my way through. I push harder, ignoring the pain, my hind paws climbing up along the webbing, claws clutching at the wire, gap by gap, then kicking, thrusting the rest of me forward until my tummy reaches the hole. It sticks, almost too big to clear the opening I've made, but I am determined.

I use my front paws to reach down on the outside of the webbing, pulling myself while my hind paws kick and climb, until finally my tummy moves through the hole, and my narrower hips and skinny legs easily slip through behind it. Now there is nothing to hold onto as I hurtle headfirst toward the ground. The fall is farther than any jump I've ever made, as far as a drop from a pygmy palm tree, but I manage to thrust out my legs and right myself as I careen through the air. I drop on my paws to the grass below…and then, as fast as I can run, I am gone.

CHAPTER THREE

Under the Deck Cat

I gallop across an open lot, my stubby legs pumping and my bell jingling, jump over a low cement wall, and race past a huge house. It is the color of the inside of a conch shell, the brilliant hue of the last rays of the sun as it sets over the water. Beyond the conch house sits an old wood and stone house, equally large, and then another building, bigger still, perched on the rocky point at the end of the island. Some of the wood is beginning to crumble on the last building, and its windows, which look in on a big open room, are cracked. By the time I reach this building, I am panting. I have never run this far or this fast!

And this time, I am running not out of blind fear or compulsion, but with the joy of freedom. The humans did not carry me outside, like last time. This time, it *was* my choice: I clawed my way out. My mother would be so proud of me! I feel exhilarated but nervous, here on the very furthest tip of the island, where she never brought us. It is strange and unknown territory, and I am all alone. I will have to muster all the skills my mother showed me, in order to survive. Still, this is better than being prisoner in that house with the talk of poison, not knowing when the woman called Darcie will return.

I snuggle against the building's cool, stone wall to rest and to study my surroundings. A tangle of matted grass and bougainvillea stretches down to the ocean, a brilliant mix of colors that flash like the eyes of the lightest cats. Large flat rocks form stepping-stones out into the surf. Fish jump in the shallows and seagulls swoop down to catch them, their beaks breaking the water as the silver backs of the fish catch the rays of the rising sun, fatal bursts of light. A huge gray heron scouts for food along the shore, his talons working through clumps of sea grass that have washed up on the beach. Overhead in the palm trees, swallows and bananaquits greet the daylight with their bird songs. From the rain gutter above me, a pair of mourning doves begins to coo. Lizards lap up the bugs that crawl along the scaevola hedges. A lone hermit crab, laboriously dragging the scavenged snail shell that serves as his current armor, makes his way to the gnarled trunk of a gumbo-limbo tree to find shade and shelter for the day.

There is not a human in sight. The building, in fact, looks abandoned, unkempt, as does its neighbor. The conch colored house, though, is apparently lived-in; chairs and tables sit on its porches, and chaises line the beach. But the house is quiet. Its occupants are probably still sleeping, or perhaps they are not here now. Either way, with only the soothing, familiar animal sounds around me, I feel safe and comforted. I take a last look at the beach, reassuring myself that I am too big now to be breakfast for the heron, and then I rest my frazzled front paws together on the ground, lower my chin onto them, and close my eyes.

A combination of hunger and warmth awaken me. The sun is high in the sky, and the ends of the fur on my back are hot as the sun's rays have settled into them. My stomach is growling. It is empty, drained from the day and night of clawing at the screen to escape, when I did not touch the food or water. I stand, stretch and look around me once again. The heron is gone and the fishing has ceased. The birds, the lizards and even the bugs are quiet. It is the silence of midday on our tropical island, when every creature tries to escape the fierce-ness of the sun.

My hunger pangs are a grim reminder that for the first time in my life, there is no one to feed me. No mother's milk, no prizes from her hunts, no food from the hands of humans. No one even to guide me toward a possible place to find lunch, no experienced nose to sniff out a hint of food. The challenge of being on my own overwhelms me and causes the hunger pangs to worsen, gripping my insides. I have never hunted for myself; I don't know if I can. And if the only thing to eat here is prey, I don't know whether I will be able to find it or catch it, let alone kill it.

This much is certain, however: I will not find food by simply standing here. I slink along the side of the building, hoping to come upon a trash can or a scrap of something edible. If I could just find food that is ready to eat, it would make my task much easier. My bell tinkles as I walk, and I realize dejectedly that if I have to hunt, the bell will warn my prey. I stop and jerk my head from side to side, violently trying to shake off the collar, but it stays put. I claw at it, futilely. It will not loosen its grip on my throat, and I give up. I lift my head and twitch my nose, but there is no scent of food in the air, so I duck under the scaevola hedge, to look for lizards still active in its shade. A tiny gecko scampers among pebbles, fragments of shell, and clods of dirt, and I stoop down to study his movements, keeping myself still. The lizard doesn't appear to notice me; he has staked out a small area, looking for bugs among the debris, intent on his work. I think of my mother and make my move, just as she used to do: a quick spring forward, a fast slap of my paw at the lizard's back. But I am not as fast as my mother: the gecko scampers away, runs up the vines of the scaevola, and disappears, camouflaging himself in the leaves.

I emerge, disheartened, from the scaevola hedge and tear toward the conch colored house, nervous out in the open.

When I reach its beachside porch, I huddle down next to the boards. It is still quiet here, and there is still no scent of lunch. I crave familiar territory, somewhere that I know I can find trash, at least. I jump back over the low stone wall and hurry across the open lot. My hunger travels with me, ripping at my stomach. When I reach the edge of the lot, I crawl under another scaevola hedge. This hedge parallels the wall of the garage where Tevin put my cage. From where I am, I can see the bathroom window from which I made my escape. The window is taller than a grown human's head! No wonder it felt like I tumbled so far! And the hole, with its frayed wires sticking out in the air like spider's legs, is so tiny that it reminds me how small I am to have fit through there.

Between the hedge and the house is a driveway. On the other side of the driveway is a low wooden deck on which sits a big, shiny grill that humans use for cooking. I contemplate jumping up on the grill. There might be fragments of food stuck to its surface. But even when I crane my neck and tilt my head all the way back, I can't see the top. It is too high for me. Part of the way up, though, is a shelf. A tool that humans use for cooking rests on the shelf. It is big and flat and looks lightly burned and crusted, as though with morsels of food. I aim myself toward the shelf, jump with all the gusto I can muster, and miss. Completely. I fall to the deck, stare up at the shelf, and sniff toward the tool, trying to detect any odor of something edible.

I decide I'll have better luck looking for lizards again. I scoot back under the hedge and sink down on all my paws to wait silently until another appears. It doesn't take long. This lizard is massive, as long as a full grown swallow, and plump— the dark kind that spends a lot of time on palm trees, his scales picking up the deep tints of the tree bark. He is so large that the claws on his webbed feet make a scrunching sound on the dried leaves carpeting the ground. He is hunting bugs and doesn't see or hear me as he works his way to within a leg length of my front paws. I fold my ears against my head and whop my tail to and fro, readying myself, and then—pounce! My paw makes perfect contact, and I quickly extend my claws to hold on to him.

The lizard squiggles and wriggles underneath my paw, frantically trying to get away, dropping his tail in the process. The thick, discarded tail wiggles on the ground like a worm, but I am not fooled. My mother showed us this lizard trick—how they drop their tails to distract you, fool you into thinking that the tail is separate prey, so that the lizard can slip out of your grasp. I clutch him firmly. And I don't bother batting him around, tossing him into the air, or waiting for him to go unconscious or die of shock—the usual ways to turn a lizard into a meal. Instead, I hold him down tight to the ground, crunch right into his belly, and eat him with his heart still beating. I am so ravenous that I even eat his head, the least tasty part of a lizard.

I am licking my paws clean, still under the scaevola hedge, when I hear the sound of boat motors, and then Tevin comes out of the garage and walks hurriedly toward the beach, his feet so close that they kick sand into the hedge. My heart races as I dash across the driveway and flatten myself against the house, scouting for a hiding place. The grill deck backs up to a flight of steps that reach from the yard to the upstairs sleeping rooms; the landing for the stairs is an old slab of concrete, and the deck surface sits two or three full-grown cat heights higher than the landing. This space, between concrete landing and wooden deck, has been left open, not boarded up. I dart through the opening and underneath the deck, all the way back, working my way around bits of concrete and lumber, construction debris that no one ever hauled away.

It is dark in here, but my vision quickly adjusts. Bits of glass, old seashells, and a couple of dead crabs litter the crawl space's sandy floor. The sharp tips of exposed nails hang down from the deck above. The boards of the deck are old and dried out by the sun, shrunken and warped, and spaces have opened up between them, whiskers wide. Through these spaces I can see glimmers of sun, and now I can hear voices getting closer to the house. They are a mix of male and female.

"Wow! What a great beach!" a man says. "I think this is the whitest sand I've ever seen!"

"Yes, it's a paradise. Can you believe how blue the water is?" a woman asks.

"Wonder how warm it gets this time of year?" another male voice says.

Apparently the boat has pulled right up onto the beach and let these people off. Then I hear her voice—the woman called Darcie. She is walking up to the garage, just steps away from me, talking excitedly with Tevin. He sounds dismayed, distressed, and a little bit defensive. She sounds as though she is trying to stay calm, to keep the anger out of her voice. They are talking about me.

"We put her in the bathroom so we could clean the house. She left just this morning, just this morning!" Tevin is saying. "All this time we take care of her, feed her, keep her safe, and just the day you are coming, she runs away!"

"But you left her in the bathroom for the whole entire night, not just long enough to clean the house," the woman answers him.

"Yes, that is true. That is true," Tevin admits.

"I can't talk about this right now," says the woman, her voice tight. "I need to take the boys inside." I hear Fred and Frisco's bells, but cannot see them in their carrier.

"Come on, folks, I'll show you to your rooms," the

woman says, and I hear a chorus of okays and thank yous from the other voices. I hold myself as still as a cracked conch shell, while they all walk by the deck no farther than a palm frond's length from me, then through the garage and into the house. I hear Tevin mutter a human's bad word under his breath as he heads to the beach; then he trudges back and forth, back and forth, bringing luggage and groceries up from the boat. Ginger comes out to help him, and I hear her ask, "Darr-say mad about Lucy?"

"Do not talk to me about that now, woman!" Tevin retorts, and tromps off through the sand again.

I figure that Tevin and Ginger are probably mad at each other, and the woman called Darcie is probably mad at both of them, and it's all because I got away. Meanwhile, here I am, practically right underneath their feet, driven back by my search for food—and I am still hungry, scared and alone. I stay down on my haunches, trying to calm myself, when suddenly there are voices again. This time, they are calling my name.

"Lucy! Lucy Miracle!" It is the woman called Darcie. She is walking within a peacock tail's length of the deck, heading toward the front lawn. "She can't be that far away," she says to someone. "She's so small; she just couldn't have gotten very far." She sounds anxious, as though she is trying to believe what she's saying.

"How big is the island?" asks a deep male voice.

"Not very big," the woman answers. "Two-and-a-half miles long and a half mile wide. Still, that's plenty of space for a tiny kitten to get lost in."

"I hope nothing got *her*," says the male voice.

"Oh, I don't think so, Douglas," the woman answers. "There aren't really any natural predators here, except the herons and egrets, and I think she's too big for them. She could get hit by a golf cart, I guess, but that's not very likely. There are some construction vehicles around these days—but most of those are so big and noisy that a cat would hear them and get out of the way."

"Hmm," the man named Douglas answers, unenthusiastically. "What about people? Do you think anyone would nab her for themselves?"

"Well, there are only about eighty homes, and everyone's here only part-time, so I don't think anyone would be interested in scooping up a cat as a full-time pet. I can't imagine that she'd go to anyone, anyway—she's still pretty feral. Probably the worst thing that could happen to her is that somebody who doesn't like cats would hurt her."

"But this island is all about cats, isn't it?" Douglas asks. "Cat Cay? I mean, even the logo's a cat on a key."

"True, but don't let that mislead you. The logo's just a play on words. I don't think anyone really knows how the island got its name. There's one story that says it's named after a cat line on a pirate ship. But Ray thinks it's probably named after a cat *rig*—the sail on a cat boat, which is a boat pirates would have liked because it goes so fast. The mast is forward, almost in the bow of the boat, and when the sail is deployed, it has about the same shape as Cat Cay.

"Legend has it that pirates were the first to use the island because they found potable water here. And the pirates might also have been the source of the cats; they would have had cats on their boats as mousers. At any rate, there are plenty of people around here who consider the cats to be nuisances."

Oh, I think to myself. No wonder the humans care so little for us; the island is not named for cats, after all. We're just accidental residents, maybe even castoffs from ships.

"Darr-say?" calls Ginger, and I hear her heavy footsteps heading toward the other voices.

"Yes?" the woman called Darcie answers.

"I have something to tell you," Ginger says. She sounds hesitant, troubled.

"Right now?" the woman asks. "Or can it wait? We're looking for Lucy."

"Well, it might be about Lucy...sort of."

"Really?" the woman asks, an uptick in her voice. "Have you seen her?"

"No, no," Ginger answers, with a nervous chuckle. There is a pause, and I imagine Ginger standing there playing with her hair, pushing it back out of her face, the way I've seen her do as she contemplates one of my messes. I think I hear her fingernail click against an earring, probably one of the bright dangly hoops she favors. "Someone is trapping cats. I was going to tell you."

"Trapping cats?" the woman repeats. "What do you mean, trapping cats?"

"He is making his worker catch the cats," Ginger answers. "He doesn't like cats. He is telling his worker to poison them."

"Poison them! Whom are you talking about?" asks the woman, her voice sharper than before.

Ginger says a name that makes my whiskers bristle as I hunch down harder into my hiding place. My muscles stiffen. I've heard other humans talk about the man called Uberan—and my mother taught us about him, too. He lives on the end of the island where I was born, and he would love to kill us all. His property is marked along the road by a tall wall of abnormally dense shrubbery. You can't see through it, but my mother thrust her paws through to show my siblings and me that on the other side of the shrubbery is barbed wire, tightly strung to keep out intruders. All we had to do was listen, to learn that the man who lives behind it doesn't like cats. He was always alone, isolated by the roadside barrier, and you could sometimes hear him holler, "*Scat!*" Then there would be the sound of water gushing out of a hose or—scarier still—the thud of a shovel whacking at the ground. It was the man, chasing cats away.

My mother was determined to teach us to ignore our curiosity and never ever break through the roadside barrier into the man's yard. It was tempting, because the shrubbery wall was so long that it seemed to promise a vast and fertile hunting ground if a cat could wiggle under it. So, my mother sniffed along the barricade until she found a hidden, shallow trench that smelled of other cats. She led us into the trench, telling us to stay with a firm meow and a swat of her paw on each of our heads. We looked around the yard. There were no garbage cans full of treats. Instead, there was a fire pit filled with smoking trash. We could smell food scraps burning in there, too. The rest of the massive yard was empty—no furniture for a cat to hide under, no soft cushions on which to sneak a nap. There were no fountains or flowerpots, no decorative shells in the yard, no place to collect rainwater for cats to drink.

Then, with another round of warning swats to our skulls, my mother left the trench and squirmed underneath the wire. She snuck quietly into the yard, keeping low and close to the towering hedge. But it was almost as though the man could smell a cat because suddenly there was the loud bang of a door slapping open and the familiar sound of "*Scat!*" as the man came running toward her, swinging a broom. My mother turned to run back toward us, her legs kicking frantically, the man flailing the broom toward her tail. He was almost upon her when another door opened and a Bahamian yelled, "Mister Uberan!" My mother's pursuer halted his chase and looked back toward the house, screaming "*What?*"

My mother ducked down under the shrubbery and

dragged herself to safety beside us, in her haste ignoring the jagged ends of the wire. They left long scratches, and we saw blood as she bathed herself afterwards.

"You're kidding!" the woman called Darcie exclaims. "He's so quiet and keeps to himself. I can't imagine him hurting a cat. Are you sure?"

"Yeesss," Ginger answers, in her deep, drawn-out way. "I am sure. Freeman tell me so."

"Freeman…he's the Bahamian caretaker, right?"

"Yess. I see him the other day. He tell me that he's supposed to trap the cats and kill them."

"Which cats?" the woman asks, her voice becoming sharper.

"Any cats that come in his yard," Ginger answers.

"And is that what he's doing?"

"No…not yet. And Freeman doesn't want to. His wife has cats in Nassau. He likes cats. But when his boss comes back to the island, Freeman will have to do what he says or else he will be fired."

"And when is his boss coming back…do we know?"

"No…he may be here now, I don't know," Ginger answers slowly, and I imagine her shrugging her shoulders.

"Well, will you please go find Freeman and ask him to come down here and see me as soon as possible," the woman commands. "Tell him that if he has any trapped cats, to bring them here with him. Tell him *not* to kill any cats. We'll take care of the cats."

"Okay," Ginger answers, and I hear her walk back toward the garage.

"Uh-oh," the man named Douglas says, and he resumes the call for me—his voice much throatier than the woman's: "Lucy! Lucy Miracle!"

"Luuuuucy…" the woman calls, and I can hear her distress.

It mirrors mine, at Ginger's news. I am tempted to leave my solitary refuge and run toward the woman called Darcie, hurling myself at her legs. "Oh, Lucy, there you are, my darling," she would say, with relief and delight. She would stoop and pick me up, cuddle me against her chest, and carry me inside the house to safety, and to food. But that would be the end of my freedom, and I would not be able to search for my mother. I hope my mother is still staying away from that man. I hope that she is not so desperately hungry that she has wiggled under his hedge again. Somehow, I should tell her of his plan to poison cats. Maybe she and I could find a way to warn the other cats. I stay put beneath the deck.

The voices fade as the woman and Douglas walk through the front lawn and then across the street. When I can no longer hear them, I figure they have disappeared behind the scaevola lining the opposite beach. There is a long stretch of silence, lengthy enough that I decide to venture out again. If I could get back under that hedge, I might be able to catch another lizard or two, enough to quiet my stomach. I did pretty well with that last lizard! And the better I become at hunting, the easier it will be for me to stay outside on my own.

I stand up underneath the deck and creep slowly toward the opening. When I get close, I again hear the sound of footsteps. Tevin rounds the corner of the house in front of me, and in panic, I turn and run as fast as I can back to the far corner of the crawl space. In my haste, I forget the bell. It jingles, and just like that, gives me away.

"Lucy!" Tevin exclaims. "I hear you! Lucy! Is that you?"

I can hear his thick shoes rushing toward my deck. He is coming to get me—he will grab a rake or a shovel and prod underneath the deck to scare me out of hiding, or he will pry up the boards above my head until I am exposed. But no—instead, he steps right *onto* the deck and hurries across it with a heavy gait, shaking the boards above my head. Then he jumps off the deck, and I hear him run through the garage to the interior door of the house. Its hinges make a low moaning sound as he opens it and hollers, "Ray! Ray!"

Moments later, the door opens again, briskly this time. I hear footsteps head toward my deck and onto it. The boards creak above me, and I watch first Ray's, and then Tevin's feet as they step down off the deck onto the concrete landing and walk along the hedge toward the bathroom window.

Ray calls my name this time. "Lucy? Lucy Miracle? Are you here?"

"I heard her, I know I heard her," Tevin tells Ray.

"Shh!" Ray says. "Listen for her bell."

I stay as still as a clamshell, hoping to keep my hiding place a secret.

I see Ray squat down to look underneath the hedge. Tevin's feet pace back and forth. Ray calls again. "Luuuuuucy! Luuuuuucy! Lucy Miracle!" He makes his voice low and syrupy, beckoning, like the cry of a mourning dove to her young ones. He is concentrating on the hedges that surround the deck and driveway. I hear him shake the scaevola leaves as he calls my name. "Luuucy Miracle…"

Ouch! A mosquito takes a sudden fierce bite that feels like a sharp kitten claw piercing the delicate underside of my ear. Without thinking, I swat at it, shaking my head and batting my ear in one quick motion that sets my bell jangling and prompts Tevin to start shouting: "Here! Here! Under the deck! She is under the deck!"

"Where?" Ray asks, excitedly.

"Under here!" Tevin answers. The boards shudder as he steps onto the deck. "I heard her bell from under here!"

"Shh!" Ray orders again. "Let's listen."

My body is trembling with fear, hunger and confusion.

I watch Ray lower himself onto his side and lie down at the opening to my hiding place, his form a dusky silhouette against the daylight as he peers into the darkness. Humans need lights to see in the dark; I know that Ray's naked eyes cannot find me in the gloom, and yet I am as cornered as a bird backed up against a tree trunk, unable to make a move because that will only entice the predator into a chase. Like a bird, I sit still, shuddering, captured once again, flimsy boards the only barrier between me and the humans who would cage me.

"Lucy?" Ray coos again. "Luuuucy…don't you want to come out, little girl?"

I stay crouched and motionless, my bell silent for many long breaths, as Ray seems to wait for me to answer him with a move or a meow. When I don't, rather than reach for me or pry the boards or try to startle me into a frightened run, Ray and Tevin, incredibly, decide to leave me alone.

Ray's shoes scrape along the concrete as he hauls himself up. "Well, let's tell Darcie, and we'll bring her some food," he says to Tevin.

My gnawing stomach surges in disbelief and craving as Tevin answers, "Okay, sir," and they walk away, over my deck, into the garage and through the groaning door to the house— the house, rich with food that you don't have to dig for or chase; food that is simply brought to you in a dish and is yours to eat without a hunt or a battle; food that is soft and warm and tastes like freshly caught fish, still salty and juicy from the ocean; food with an aroma so pungent it calls to you on the breeze; food that fills your stomach until it feels as hard and round as a coconut.

"Lucy?" a voice calls, soft as a hummingbird's wings. With a startle, I awaken. In my exhaustion and relief, I have fallen asleep, salivating to my dreams of food…and now, in the opening to my hiding place, human feet appear, the feet of the woman called Darcie, and her hand reaches down and places a small, sky-colored bowl on the concrete, and I realize that the delicious aromas are not simply in my dreams—they are real, and only a deck's width away from me.

"Lucy Miracle," the woman sings in her hummingbird voice, "here's some food for you, baby; you must be very, very hungry by now, little darling. Don't you want to come out and eat it?" And then I see her bottom settle on the concrete as she sits beside the food. She doesn't move or say anything else. My stomach and my brain begin to fight with each other like two angry roosters, thrusting and dodging. My stomach tells me to leap at the food and gobble it down. My brain holds me back, knowing that if I go to the bowl, the woman can reach out and grab me as easily as a lizard laps up a hapless ant.

I wait.

She waits.

My nose twitches in torture at the smell of tuna.

She sits and waits.

My stomach snarls.

She sits and waits.

Saliva drizzles down my whiskers.

She sits and waits.

The light at the opening grows dimmer; dusk is settling in.

She waits.

My paws flex. They are ready to move.

A door opens; I hear it squeal gently and brush the air as it swings wide. Human voices spill out from the house into the yard, and then Tevin's voice calls loudly, "Dinner is served."

"Okay," the woman calls back. "I'll be right there. Tell everyone else to sit."

"Yes, ma'am," answers Tevin.

"Well, little girl," the woman says, softly again, "I guess

you don't want to come out right now. That's okay. I'll just leave this food for you, and you can eat it when you're ready. I'm going to go enjoy my own dinner. You have a lovely night. I'll be back to visit you in the morning."

My stomach surges once again, and as soon as the woman's footsteps fade into the garage and I hear the door moan closed, I charge toward the bowl. Sinking my face into it, I gobble the shredded fish as though it were liquid, not taking the time to chew, just swallowing the luscious stuff whole, gulp, gulp, gulp, a low growl rumbling instinctively in my throat to warn off competition. Then I lick and lick and lick the bowl, gathering every last drop of juice, every ant-sized speck of food.

When I am done, I amble back to my corner, warmed from the inside out by the food bulging in my stomach, and feeling safely alone in the deepening dusk. With all the humans inside the house, I don't worry about the jingle of my bell as I bathe myself, licking my paw pad until it is moist, and then using the pad to wash the remnants of dinner off my face, my mouth, my nose, my whiskers.

My paw lingers, as always, on my ear—the ear that is not smooth and perfectly pointed toward the sky like the other, but has a missing piece at the top tip, like the notch between the branches of a ficus tree. It is the mark of a cat that has been captured and operated on, a cat who cannot make kittens. When I first understood this, it seemed cruel to me, like just another way to kill off the island cats, only more slowly than poisoning or drowning or shooting. But then I heard the woman called Darcie explain that humans think it's a kindness to do this to us. She said it means fewer mouths to feed—so cats don't have to struggle as desperately as my mother did, gathering enough nutrition to nurse their litters, when the mothers are nearly starving themselves. I think of my mother, kittenless now, as I take special care to reach down into the notch where the fur still sprouts up like grass, and clean it carefully. Finally, the rhythm of my bathing, the fullness of my stomach, the quiet and darkness of my haven lull me into sleep again.

When I awaken, it is night, whispers of moonlight seeping through the cracks in the deck, the rustle of hermit crabs lugging their borrowed shells, the plaintive low meow of a cat in the distance. I ache for my mother, my littermates, the warmth and consolation of their bodies beside me, their companionship. Rather than languish here in my loneliness, I decide to take advantage of the darkness and go for a solitary stroll.

Emerging from underneath the deck, I see that the moon is nearly full, blazing in the sky like a cat's eye, bright enough to cast shadows underneath my paws as I head out on the same path I took at sunrise, after my jump from the bathroom window. This time though, I am not frantic or afraid, and I take my time, stopping to gnaw at a tall blade of grass wet with evening dew, rubbing my chin, paws and rump on trees and bushes, leaving my scent to mark my way and to claim my territory, as my mother taught me. Under the trees at the edge of the driveway, I step around fallen coconuts, far bigger than I am, slowly turning dark. The grass in the open field feels almost matted, spongy yet coarse to the paw, and it is mottled with tiny burrs that aren't so much painful as they are a nuisance, grabbing onto my feet and forcing me to stop and chew them out.

Just as in the day, the conch-colored house is quiet, no lights on, its porches with the tables and chairs sitting quietly upright and at the ready, like herons on the lookout. As I round the house, I see a flash of fur, the back end of a cat slinking away. The fur looks fluffier than mine. Did this cat run from me, or was she simply headed in that direction?

Would a stranger cat see me as an intruder, or as a possible companion? I peer around the corner looking for answers, but the cat is gone.

On I walk, to the old wood and stone house, looking even more enormous in the dark than in the daylight. I continue to the next wood and stone building, out on the point, and peer through its cracked windows. In the big open room, I see lots of round tables. Chairs sit on top of the tables, upended, their legs extending into the air like uplifted human arms. Cobwebs spill from the chairs to the tables. Around the other side of the building, next to the water, is a patio—the kind of space where humans like to have parties, enjoying their drinks and the island sunshine while they watch the waves break over the rocks in the distance. The patio is separated from the ocean by a tall glass wall. Sea spray sprinkles the glass, which is mildewed and cloudy with age and in some spots completely shattered by the wind.

I sniff along the edges of this patio; I can smell cats, although none that I recognize. There is a particularly strong scent, musky like the intentional harsh spray of a tomcat, and I follow it warily along the edge of the building. I have to creep beneath the bushes that line the building to track the scent, and when I raise myself to turn a corner, a branch that had been hugging the ground catches inside my collar and rises, with me attached to it!

I wiggle my neck, trying to break free, but I am caught on the branch, my collar tying me to it. Shaking my head from side to side does nothing but make me dizzy, and slides the branch further inside my collar. I can feel its ragged end poking into my shoulder. What I need to do is slowly back off the branch, hoping that it will slide out of my collar as I back up—but after a few steps, I grow impatient and throw all of my feet backwards in unison, while whipping my neck up into the air, a quick jerking movement that works a miracle: my collar pops open at the clasp and falls to the ground, its bell offering a final violent rattle as it hits the dirt.

I stare at the collar in astonishment, the symbol of my captivity lying useless in the dust. I gallop across the patio, right down the middle of it in the dark. The only noise I make is the light smack of paws against stone. I run to a coconut tree and thrust my front claws into it, scratching vigorously, sharpening them on the tree bark. I throw my head back and let loose a low, throaty growl at the coconuts above. The strength of my voice startles me—I had not been using it in captivity or in hiding. My voice seems to be growing along with my body! I growl again: *grrrr!* I rush away from the tree and dash across the grass, kicking up my paws, meowing and growling. Finally, I nestle against a hedge, winded.

I sit there catching my breath. From somewhere down the road, a familiar sound, traveling on the wind, breaks the stillness of the night. It is the sound of a trash can toppling over. I hear its lid bounce along the road and twirl into silence as it comes to rest. Then the rustling of papers, the scrape of cans, the clink of bottles being batted about. A cat, scavenging for a midnight meal. A rat rustles past me, just beyond the hedge. Its feet sink in the grass, its nose twitches as it sniffs out bugs in the night. I hear the flap of wings and look up as an owl settles onto a tree branch, a freshly caught fish flailing in its beak.

Hunger clutches at my stomach and a force that I recognize washes over me, like sand and shells mixed with seaweed in a riptide, so churned up together that they are one tangled mob. I am swept along by this force; it is too strong for me to swim against or tame. It propels me away from the hedge; I gallop full speed past the conch house, over the wall, through the field, up the driveway, and back to the silence and shelter of my hideaway underneath the deck.

Panting, I realize that my eyes, almost like independent selves, are searching for the sky-colored bowl. The bowl is empty, but it is the promise of food that drove me back. When the sun rises, I will not slink under buildings or crawl beneath tree trunks or climb high into the branches to hide until another night's hunt. My bowl will be full of fresh food, brought by the woman called Darcie.

Perhaps tomorrow night I will practice my hunting. Perhaps tomorrow night I will meet another cat. Perhaps tomorrow night I will venture out in the other direction, to search for my mother. For now, I sink down on my stomach and into sleep, and dream once again.

"Rat poison," a brusque Bahamian voice says, and I realize that I am waking up. This is not a nightmare.

"Rat poison!" repeats the woman called Darcie, incredulously. The voices are coming from just next to my deck, outside the garage. "How are you supposed to do that?"

"Well, there's plenty of rat poison on the island, you know. The exterminator sets it out in rat traps…you've seen them, those black boxes with holes for the rats to crawl in? They're beside the trash cans, and in clumps of trees. They have some by the restaurant, too."

"Yes, I've seen them, Freeman," the woman called Darcie answers. "But cats can't get into those holes—they're too small. Exactly how are you supposed to get the cats to eat the poison?"

"He is bringing traps for us," the Bahamian voice answers. "We have to set the traps in the yard and put cat food in them. He told us to mix the rat poison with the cat food. The cats will go in the traps and eat the food. Then we're supposed to leave the cats in them until they die."

"Oh, no!" the woman called Darcie exclaims. "How many cats do you have in your yard?"

Fully conscious now, I understand that this is the yard my mother so vividly warned us about. I crawl closer to the voices.

"Not that many," the male voice answers. "Maybe one or two wanders through each day...sometimes we only see a few a week. But it doesn't matter. He doesn't want to see any. He hates cats—he says they have diseases and make the island dirty."

"Well, that's nonsense!" the woman fires back. "Cats are some of the cleanest animals on the planet, and our island cats don't have any diseases. We've tested them. They're just hungry, that's all—they're looking for food. That's why they're in his yard! *You* don't want to kill the cats, do you, Freeman?" she asks, more slowly.

"No, I have nothing against cats," the man answers. "My wife has two cats in Nassau. She would kill *me* if she knew I hurt a cat. But I work for him. I have to do what he says."

"Well, let's try to find a way to get you out of this. When is he coming over with the traps?" the woman called Darcie asks.

"One week. He will be here next Saturday."

"Okay, Freeman, I'll be here then. We need to come up with a plan." The woman called Darcie pauses. "How about this? Do what he says: set the traps, put the cat food inside. But *don't* put any poison in the food—just pretend that you have. Then when you catch the cats, bring them down here to us. We'll take them back to their territory and set them free—and he'll think they've been killed."

"But he told us to put them behind the shed to die," Freeman protests.

"Well, tell him that you'd rather take them away from the house. Tell him they die really fast because you're using so much poison, and you want to take them to the incinerator right away. He doesn't want to see the cats, so he won't care—right? Just as long as he thinks they're dead?"

I shiver. I hope that my mother is following her own warnings. I hope she never goes near this man, or his yard.

"You're probably right," Freeman answers. "I think I can do that. But if I were taking the cats to the incinerator, I'd be coming back with empty traps. And you want me to leave the traps here."

"You're right—but that's not a problem. I'll get out some of the traps that we used when we spayed and neutered the cats. You can take *them* back, instead. They all look the same."

"All right, okay, I guess that will work."

"Should I talk to him?" the woman called Darcie asks. "Do you think he would listen to me if I asked him not to kill the cats?"

"No, I don't think it would do any good. The only thing that'll help is to keep all the cats out of his yard, if you can think of a way to do that!"

"Well, I don't know how..." the woman called Darcie answers. "Maybe if they got enough to eat somewhere else, they would never go in his yard..." her voice trails off. When it picks up again, it is brisk, determined. "Okay, for now, here's the plan: you don't poison the food, you *do* trap the cats, and you bring them here to me. Agreed?"

"Yes," Freeman answers.

"You promise?" the woman called Darcie asks him. I hear both concern and the hint of a smile in her voice.

"Promise!" Freeman answers firmly.

"Okay, then, if he's coming in a week—next Saturday—I'll start looking for you with cats next Sunday, right?"

"Right!"

"I'll tell Ginger, and Tevin, and Ray. If I'm not here when you bring a cat, find someone else. Or if nobody's here, come into the garage. Then when it's dark, take the cat back to your end of the island and let it go yourself, okay? But remember to take an empty trap back right away, as though you've just gone to the incinerator."

"Okay," Freeman answers.

"Oh, one more thing—before you pick up a trap with a cat in it, throw a towel over the trap. It calms the cat, so it won't thrash so much. And it won't be able to get at you if it's trying to claw or bite—although most of them don't. They're too scared at that point. You're not afraid to carry the cats, are you, Freeman?"

"No, ma'am, I'm a big man!" he laughs. "And my skin is tough!"

"Okay then, let's shake on it," the woman called Darcie says, and I hear a swishing noise and a light clap of hands coming together.

"Done," says Freeman.

"Done," says the woman called Darcie, in a tone that I almost don't recognize. It is the sternest, most serious voice I have ever heard her use.

I hear feet walk into the garage. I scramble from under the deck, hop up on top of it, and poke my head around the wall. Freeman gets into his golf cart and pulls away. The woman called Darcie watches him, her back to me, hands on her hips. She shakes her head from side to side. She turns toward the door that leads into the house. Her hand reaches out for the knob. Her body turns slightly as she swings the door open, toward me. I back up, straight into a hapless hermit crab that clatters off the deck and onto the sidewalk below. The woman's head whips in my direction. "Lucy!" she exclaims. I hurl myself backwards off the deck and under it, before she can make another move.

Later, when the woman called Darcie comes to feed me, her hummingbird voice is back. "Luuuucy…Lucy Miracle," it flutters lightly, "I've brought your breakfast, little girl. Are you still here, baby?"

The odor of fish floats with her voice into the darkness of my hiding place. I hold myself as still as a stone. Then I remember that she can't hear me anymore, not with my bell gone, and I allow myself to creep forward, just a couple of leg lengths, to smell the food and see what the woman called Darcie is doing.

I see her arm in a flowered fabric, the colors of our ocean, reach down and place the sky-colored bowl on the concrete landing. "I brought you something different this morning—crispy cat cereal! Would you like to come out and try it, Lucy Miracle?"

I long for the food, yet I am fearful of being captured again. I do not want another collar around my neck. I do not want to be locked back in the house, or in a cage. So I resolutely settle in to wait, and so does she. When my front paws flex with impatience, I put a paw on top of the other, telling them not to move.

Several catnaps later, as the sun is warming up the day, she says, "Well, Lucy Miracle, I can't sit here all morning. I have things to do and guests to take care of. I'm sure you're hungry, so I'll just leave this food for you, okay, sweetie?" And then, as though she can read my thoughts: "I guess you're a little bit afraid to come out here, so how about if I just put the bowl inside for you? Would that be okay?"

She picks up the bowl and sets it underneath the deck, just a cat's tail length inside, to a place where I can reach it but still be under cover, and then she gets up and walks away. I don't even wait for the moan of the door this time before I race toward the meal. I lap it down voraciously. The food settles in a satisfying lump in my stomach, setting off an instinctive purr.

After I finish the last tidbit, I lick myself clean. I nap, and then awaken to her voice again. "I see you liked it, didn't you little girl?" she sings to me. "I'll come back to see you later." All through the day she returns, settling herself on the landing, talking to me or sitting quietly, before she gets up and wanders off and then comes back again. I don't know what she's up to; she's not bringing food and she's not trying to capture me. She doesn't seem to be doing anything other than idling the day away, just like a cat. When she talks, it is mostly just to repeat the name she's given me, in that singsong voice. "Lucy Miracle," she says. "Little Luuuuucy. Lucy Miracle," over and over.

Every once in a while, Ray joins her. "Any sign of her?" he'll ask. Or, "Still here?" When he asks that, I don't know whether he means me or her.

"Umhmm," she says, a patient hum in her voice.

When she's not there, I think about breaking away from under the deck, running around a bit to stretch my legs, but I don't dare. What if she were to arrive at just that moment and snatch me up?

I jump up on a conch shell. It rolls and throws me off. I walk toward the corner and find a brick. It holds steady as I hop onto it. I squint through a crack in the boards, but there is nothing to see except scaevola leaves. I step off the brick and leap onto a length of board in the far corner. It is not as big as the brick. I struggle to stay upright on my paws, teetering as I search for an opening in the wood, but the board doesn't help me find a new view at all. In the middle of my hiding space is the end of a rusted old shovel. I hop on it just for something to do. It seesaws and pitches me off. I pace, restless.

Anxiety and bewilderment keep me company underneath the deck all day long. Anxiety at the possibility of being caught again, bewilderment at my own feelings: I am restless, awaiting the woman called Darcie's visits, anxious to see her! Finally, the darkening of the cracks between the boards, the slightest cooling of the air, the rustle of lizards and crabs crawling to life, let me know that the sun is beginning to set.

Just as evening settles in, she returns a last time, carrying the bowl. My stomach jumps as she says, "Dinnertime, little girl…it's been a long day, you must be hungry. I even warmed it up for you tonight, Lucy Miracle." She sets the bowl on the landing, and sits down on the other side of it. The tantalizing aroma steams into the air. I do not budge. We both sit soundlessly and wait.

Later, long enough to have eaten several dinners, she moves the bowl a tail's length inside my deck. "I'm going to go eat my own dinner now, sweet thing," she says. "I'll be back to see you in the morning. You have a good night, little darling." And then she is gone, and I am eating again.

Thus the pattern of my life as a deck cat is set.

Each time the woman called Darcie visits, the bowl calls out to me. And while she waits beside it, the woman does the strangest things: you would swear, if you couldn't plainly see that she is human, that the woman is a cat.

She lies down on her back and stretches her body out in that long, languid way we cats love. She reaches her arms toward the lawn, stretching her fingertips, her legs extended toward the deck with her toes pointed, and then she waves her fingers and toes like cat feet clawing through the thick island air. She rolls her head from side to side, her cheeks pausing on the pavement, like a cat marking with its scent glands. She wiggles her bottom and her back on the cement, as though trying to soak up the heat of the sun that has settled there. She makes soft, contented noises, a hum deep in her throat, almost like a purr. Sometimes she rolls over onto her stomach, still purring, limbs still extended, then raises herself up onto her hands and knees, like a cat coming to its feet. Sometimes she stops her stretching and rolling, curls up in a ball, and takes a little catnap, putting her chin on her hands just the way we cats rest on our paws.

Sometimes she even meows! I can't catch her meaning—it sounds like nonsense to me—and I don't know whether she is talking to herself or trying to talk to me. But as I watch and listen to this every day, a longing starts to grow inside me, way down in the depths of my contented stomach, just below my lonely heart. It is a longing to step boldly into the sunshine, to stretch myself out beside her and feel the heat of the toasted cement. It is a longing to flex and arch my body as she does, to snuggle up beside her, to lick her face, to knead her belly. And she would pet me. I remember the feel of her hands, the caress of the baby wipes on my skin.

Still, like the squawking seagull who swoops hungrily down yet can't quite bring himself to take the bread offered by an outstretched hand, I creep toward the opening, raise a tentative paw to take that first step—and draw back! It's too close, she's too close, I'm too close, my heart starts to pound, my breath gets short, and my whiskers close in against my face. Fear sends me slinking backwards again, into my safety and solitude.

Until I hear the woman called Darcie cry.

The sound of scraping metal jolts me into alertness. It's a sound I am acquainted with. There's a dull clank as the metal hits the garage floor. Then the groan of the door.

"Happy Sunday," I hear the woman called Darcie call. "I guess the dirty work has started, has it, Freeman?"

"Yes, ma'am, I'm afraid it has," he answers. He sounds distressed.

"Is everything okay?" the woman called Darcie asks, her voice suddenly apprehensive. "I take it there's a cat under that towel, right? One that you got out safely?"

"Yes, Miss Darcie—a big one," Freeman answers.

I poke my head out and think about jumping up onto the deck to peek around the corner of the garage. I want to see the cat in the trap. The woman called Darcie and Freeman are busy; maybe they won't notice me.

"Well, great. Let's carry the trap into the side yard," the woman called Darcie says, and I stay put. "We'll set it under the trees, so the cat will have some cover and can feel at least a little bit protected until I take him down and let him go."

"Okay," Freeman says again. I hear the scuff of metal as the trap is lifted off the floor, and then their footsteps walk by my deck as they head toward the grass. The footsteps fade. When they return, the woman called Darcie is talking. She sounds upset.

"*Dead?* How?" she asks, her voice rising.

Freeman mentions the name that makes my whiskers bristle. "He was all fired up when he got here yesterday," Freeman says. "Took out the traps first thing and showed me how to set them up and use them. He was so excited that he dished up the bait himself: tuna fish. And then he put the rat poison in the food."

"Oh, no! Did you know he put the poison in?"

"Yes I did, I watched him. He stirred in a lot. Then we set the traps around the yard. And he didn't stop there—he put traps in the lot next door, too."

"The lot next door? That field that's not cleared, all full of weeds and trees? Is that Uberan's lot, too?"

"Yes, it is. I tried to talk him out of putting traps there…

told him they'd be too hard to get to. But he knows that cats hang out in that lot—all the undergrowth is good shelter for them and probably good hunting, too. So I couldn't change his mind."

Oh, no! I think. My mother! She goes in that lot sometimes...I don't think she'll expect danger there.

"After we got done setting all the traps and he went in the house," Freeman continues, "I went around to the traps by myself and changed out the bait. I put in fresh tuna and burned the poisoned food in the fire pit. But somehow, I must have missed one trap." Freeman's voice catches. He stops talking and takes a long, halting breath. "When I went to check the traps this morning, we'd caught two cats. And one of them was dead. I'm so sorry, Miss Darcie, I didn't mean for this to happen."

I hear a rustle of fabric and the sound of the woman's hand patting Freeman. "Oh, Freeman, I know you didn't," she comforts him. "It wasn't your fault. But are the traps in the yard still set?"

"Yes, they are," Freeman answers.

"And are you absolutely sure there's no rat poison in the rest of the food?"

"Yes, ma'am, I am. I went around to every trap and changed the food again, and this time I counted and double-counted. I'm sure."

"Okay, Freeman, you did the best you could," she tells him. "What did you do with the dead cat?"

"Well, Miss Darcie, I meant to leave him at the incinerator. But when I looked at all those cans full of trash waiting to be burned, I just couldn't bear to put him in a bag and leave him there," Freeman says, with grief in his voice. "And I couldn't take him home and bury him—I might have gotten caught. So I brought him down here to you."

"That's fine," says the woman called Darcie. "I'm glad you

did. We'll bury him," she says. "Where is he?"

"He's right here in my cart, wrapped up," Freeman answers.

"Let me have him," she says.

I hear a light swoosh, and then a pause. I pitch my ears all the way forward. "Oh, my God!" the woman called Darcie cries. "He's just a baby." I hear her voice catch, and then I hear sniffles. "I'm sorry, Freeman, I just can't help it," she says. "It's too sad. He's only a tiny baby. He couldn't have been more than a few months old, out on his own. Look how thin he is."

She chokes on her words, and I creep out of my crawlspace and across the deck. I push my face around the garage wall, just far enough to see her. She is sitting on the garage floor, cradling a kitten smaller than I am. The kitten is the color of tree bark, with the palest of whiskers. His head lies limp in the crook of the woman's elbow. Tears run down her cheeks as she stares at the kitten's face. She is stroking his lifeless head.

"We can't let this happen again, Freeman," she says, lifting her wet face to look up at him. Freeman is a slim, dark Bahamian, towering over her. His face is dry, but his eyes are damp, and they look almost as sad as hers.

"I know, Miss Darcie," he says. "I am so sorry. I will not let it happen again. I've hidden the rat poison so that he can't find it, and I told him I would bait the traps myself from now on. I even showed him this dead cat, so he would believe it's working. And I promise, I will bring you every cat we trap, as soon as I can."

"Okay Freeman, thank you," she answers, standing up. She is still cradling the kitten in her arms. From one hand, an old towel dangles. "I'll see that this one gets a proper burial. Now you go on home and watch out for all the other cats, okay?"

"Okay," Freeman answers, and as he walks toward his golf cart I fight an impulse to leap into the garage and go to the woman called Darcie, brush up against her legs and comfort her. But she is holding a dead kitten. I remember my mother's lessons and bustle back under the deck.

Later, I hear Tevin shoveling, somewhere just beyond the scaevola hedge. Scrape, thap. The shovel digs into the ground and dumps a pile of dirt. Scrape, thap. I venture away from my hiding place to get a better view. Looking around to make sure that no one can see me, I dart across the driveway and hop up onto a low branch. As I start to lose my balance, I sink my claws into the branch to stop myself from falling and settle down on my paws for stability. From here, I can see Tevin at work. The woman called Darcie waits beside him. He doesn't need a very big hole. I hear Darcie say good-bye to the kitten as she places him in the earth. I open my mouth to offer a good-bye meow, but no sound comes out.

The sun is already sinking in the sky when Darcie comes to my landing. But this time is different: she brings the cat called Fred with her. She sits on the warm cement, cuddling him. She pets his fur with great long strokes from head to tail. He lifts his back to meet her hand, his bell tinkling gently as his head rises to nuzzle her chest. She kisses him on the nose, the eyes, the ears. He nips at her nose, gentle little nips of affection. He leaves his scent all over her: her legs, her arms, her hands. He purrs as he rubs against her with the glands of his face and paws—even the glands next to his tail—to mark her as his own. Then he licks himself, lapping up their inter-mingled scents, purring and talking. His meows tell Darcie how much he is enjoying their time together. "Meeo*www*... meeo*www*....meeo*www*," he says, his voice scratchy and rising to a chirp at the end.

As I watch them nuzzle, I realize that I have crept so close to the opening of the deck that my whiskers are beginning to blow in the breeze. But I do not retreat. Instead, I flare my nostrils and open my mouth, inhaling the scents of human and cat together as I stare, fascinated by their interaction.

With the very next sunrise, I begin a journey down a passageway that seems to lead in only one direction, an inevitable route—like when you scamper under a hedge, not knowing what lies behind it, so intent on catching the lizard you're chasing that you forget to care. The lizard leading you onward is all that you can see.

Darcie brings my breakfast, cooing like a mourning dove. "Good morning, little Lucy Miracle," she says. "What a lovely morning, isn't it?"

She sits down and sets the bowl on the concrete, right next to her. I gallop straight at it, with no more hesitation than a pelican diving into a school of ballyhoo. My throat swelling like a pelican's as it swallows the fish whole, I guzzle the meal as quickly as I can.

When I finish the final morsel, I turn to run, but something pounces on the back of my neck with the swiftness and surety of that same pelican. It picks me up at my nape, just like the fish out of water, straight off the ground, my legs dangling and paws flopping. I draw back my lips and bare my teeth, snarling. I thrust out my claws, wriggling and pawing frantically. But I am hanging—there is nothing to grab but air. The grip on my neck does not loosen.

My heart races as I feel myself being hauled backwards, quickly and smoothly. My entire body is turned completely around—like one of the island children's kites, whipping in the wind—and now I see a face. It is Darcie who has hold of me. She lowers me into the soft folds of the flowered fabric, against her chest, and I am captured next to her own beating heart. She releases her grip on my neck and uses both hands to clasp me to her. I pull in my claws, cover my teeth, go quiet, and cease my struggle. I do not want to hurt Darcie—and besides, my strength is no greater against hers than a seashell's against the tide. Even if I were to summon the will to escape, it would wither like a flower without rain, because I am no match for what comes next.

Darcie pets me almost ferociously. Her caresses remind me of the cleaning my mother used to give us when she returned from a successful hunt and nursed us until our bellies were full, the milk that had drizzled down my chin drying in my fur. She would lick the milk and me like the gardener's rake through island leaves, hard and fast, over and over again, her tongue alternating with little nips of her teeth to pull the knots from my fur.

The woman called Darcie rakes through my fur with her hands, from head to tail, just as I saw her do with Fred, alternating a smooth rub against the top of my fur with a scratchy one that penetrates down to the skin, tickling my flesh. She uses her fingers to nuzzle my ears, one finger outside the ear and one inside, where I can't reach, making me quiver. She grabs each of my feet in turn, spreading my toe pads and scratching in between them, squeezing at the pads until the claws come out of their own accord and stretch in pleasure.

She turns me over on my back and rubs behind my shoulder blades, her thumbs in the sockets of my front legs. My legs seem to wilt. They flap idly away from my belly, and I sway with her massage like the palm fronds in the breeze, up and down, up and down. My head goes limp, and falls backward. While I am still on my back, my body bobbing as though it has gone lifeless, she reaches around to the nape of my neck—this time to scratch it, roughly, while she bends over and gently kisses my belly.

The whole time, Darcie is purring at me with her human purr—a low sort of humming. But the humming is not wordless; it is the hum of the name she has given me, said over and over: "Lucy Miracle…little Lucy Miracle…precious Lucy Miracle…baby Lucy Miracle…"

And as for me: I have gone from mindless fear, to acquiescence at my own captivity, to pleasure at being petted, to absolute surrender, all in the time it would take to run from here to the end of the island. I realize that I, too, am purring, the deep purr of a kitten nuzzled with her littermates against her mother's breast. My paw pads are digging at Darcie's chest and I am hearing my name. Lucy Miracle is me. The frightened, lonely, nameless cat that I used to be…is gone.

CHAPTER FOUR

House Cat

A fter my petting, I feel a bit bolder and start to spend more time at the edge of my crawlspace, looking out and listening for the humans or the other cats. When I hear those sounds, I tiptoe out a little farther to watch and listen. And when there is no one around, I begin to indulge in a new luxury: I emerge from underneath my deck in broad daylight and sun myself on the landing.

I am in a deep and fearless sleep on the landing when I am awakened by the sound of humans clattering and clunking about. I can tell that something important has arrived in the garage.

The big van that makes a lot of noise pulls in—it doesn't hum like a golf cart, it roars like a boat or an airplane. The roar quiets abruptly, the van's door opens and slams, another of its doors swings open, and then Tevin, Ray and Darcie come through the groaning door from the house to the garage, all of them talking at the same time. I scamper for safety under the rim of my deck, with only my head exposed. I tilt my ears toward the garage, trying to catch every sound.

"How you doin', Dillon?" Tevin greets the driver of the van.

An unfamiliar voice answers, "All right, all right, okay, okay," in the Bahamian humans' way, and then I hear a dull, muffled scrape, as though something is being dragged out of the back of the van.

"Yes, the doghouses!" Ray says. "Thanks, man. You can pile them up right here in the garage."

DOGhouses? I think with a startle. I know that certain humans bring their dogs with them to the island, but dogs live in the *human* houses. Are we going to have dogs with their own houses now? Enough houses to pile up? Are the dogs going to live here? All the time? Right here in the garage?

"Did the cat food come, too?" Darcie asks.

"Yes, it be still at the airport. I'll go back for it," Dillon answers.

"Wonderful! Thank you," says Darcie.

I strain to tilt my ears even more, until it feels as though their roots might pull loose from the top of my head.

There are the sounds of human grunts and groans, footsteps as objects are lifted and carried, the dull clatter of the doghouses, I guess, being piled on the cement floor of the garage, one after the other. Then the van door slams shut again. "Thanks, Dillon," Ray says. "See you in a few minutes."

"All right, okay," Dillon answers, and the loud roar begins again, as sudden as thunder. The van pulls out of the garage, its nose headed right toward my deck, and I duck my head underneath the wooden slats for cover as its huge wheels swing away from me, moving just beyond the scaevola hedge around my deck and down the driveway. When its noise feels safely distant, out comes my head, up go my ears.

"…right by the construction trailer," Ray is saying. "You'll see them, a big mound of pilings left over from building the new docks. We need eight chunks cut out of those pilings, about a foot tall each, nice and smooth on the top."

"Let me get the chain saw, I go right now," Tevin says. A few footsteps, and then I hear him set the saw, with a metallic clank, into the open bed of his golf cart—the tall cart with the extra wide wheels—and then it, too, drives around my deck and away, quiet as a hummingbird in comparison to the van, and familiar enough that I don't even duck my head. Golf carts go by my deck more often than the tide changes, telling me that humans are constantly on the move, going and coming, coming and going.

"Let's get these ready to go," says Ray. "Here's a pile of plastic flaps."

"Oh good, the doors," Darcie answers him. "They'll keep out bad weather. The dog jumps in through the slit down the middle."

"I sure hope they keep out the chickens, turkeys and peacocks, like they're supposed to," Ray says. "Do you think the flaps will frighten the cats?"

"Oh no," Darcie says firmly. "As soon as they know there's food inside, they'll get used to a little bit of plastic slapping their backsides."

For a while, there is no talking, only the sound of the doghouses being put together—the scrape of the pieces being dragged across the floor, the snap of them being locked into each other, the flap of plastic against plastic, like when the wind knocks over newly emptied trash cans and they blow and roll into each other.

When the van comes back with the cat food, I sneak out from under my deck and hop on top of it. I stick my face around the corner of the house and peer into the garage.

Dillon is unloading big, shiny bags. Each has a picture of a grinning cat on it. The food inside the bags is so heavy that Dillon grunts as he lifts them out of the van.

"Let's pile these bags right on top of each other in the corner here," Ray instructs, gesturing toward the corner closest to my deck. I pull my head back and squat down so I won't be seen. There is the sound of thick paper slapping together, as bag after bag hits the pile. As they drop, they make a crackling noise, like the sound of twigs snapping. The food inside those bags must be the crunchy kind, I think, not like the soft food I usually get for breakfast and dinner. Do dogs eat crunchy cat food?

The noise stops and Ray says, "Thanks for your trouble, man." I imagine him handing Dillon money, or maybe a beer or food. I remember the way my mother, littermates and I used to hide and watch the humans offer each other things: clothes, food, drink, the paper they call money. It looked so carefree, this casual giving from hand to hand, in comparison to our daily struggle. Every hard-won scrap of food that our mother laid at our feet came at the expense of her own belly—we could not even think of turning over the precious proceeds of our hunts to anyone but close relatives whom we were trying to keep alive.

This time when the van starts up, I do not duck under the deck; I simply flatten my ears against my head, pull my whiskers in, and wait it out, watching the van go by.

Soon, Tevin pulls into the garage in his golf cart, its bed filled with short, thick chunks of wood.

"Cool," I hear Ray say. "That's just what we need. Now let's figure out what screws we're going to use."

More clattering and lifting and scraping, and then Tevin, Darcie and Ray drive by my deck, slowly. Each of them is in a separate golf cart. On the back of every cart are a couple of the houses. "Follow me," Darcie says. "I've mapped out all of the locations."

"We're right behind you!" Ray tells her.

I creep around the corner of the house and into the garage, my curiosity as insistent as my hunger used to be. The pile of bags in the corner is half a human high, each bag as long as the seat of a beach chair, each the bright colors of an evening sky. I jump, aiming for the top of the pile. My claws sink into a bag half way up, ripping it open as I slither back down, trying to hold on. I should have known the top was too high! When I hit the floor, I inspect the pile more carefully. There is a tiny ledge on each bag, sticking out below the bag stacked above it. The ledges look just big enough for my paws, if I work my way up carefully. I start at the bottom bag, balance myself, stretch my paws toward the bag above it, sink in my claws and climb up. It works! I do this bag by bag, clawing, stretching, clutching, all the way up until I *am* on top of the pile. I have never been this high before! I can see the boards that crisscross the ceiling and the wires that snake between them. Through the open garage door, I can see all the way to the ocean.

Across from me, down on the floor next to the big cold box called the freezer, is a single doghouse, the color of grass.

I make my way down the pile, hind end first, getting a fresh whiff of cat food every time I sink my claws into a bag. I cross to the doghouse. It sits upright, balanced on top of a stout log. The log is a couple of heads taller than a full-grown cat. In the doghouse doorway are the clear plastic flaps. After I sniff around for a while, I leap up and through the slit. There is room in the doghouse for a whole litter of cats my size; a couple of grown cats could get in here easily. Big screws in the floor lock the doghouse onto the log beneath it. When I jump out, it holds steady.

Too bad it's a doghouse, I think, studying it from the outside, because a cat would feel safe in there. The outside is familiar, even inviting, colored to blend in with grass and trees. Inside, it would offer shelter from the wind and rain. The house is set high enough to give a cat a good vantage point, and if she saw something—or someone—coming, she could hop out between the flaps and run away.

I decide to give the doghouse a thorough test. I jump back in and peer out through the flaps. Sure enough, I can see just fine. I lie down on the floor. It is not exactly soft, but it gives a bit beneath my body. I stretch out. A dog would have plenty of room in here. And it's comfortable. I lay my head on my paws and before I know it, I am asleep.

The sound of golf carts awakens me when the humans return, and I scamper under a workbench, out of sight—just in time. They gather around this last doghouse.

"All right then, on three," directs Ray. "One...two...three!"

Ray and Tevin carry the doghouse down the driveway. Across the road, beneath a clutch of palm trees, they drop the log that it sits on into the sand. The edges of the doghouse extend out over the log like the edges of an island dandelion drooping down over its stem, but the doghouse doesn't wobble, even though they set it down hard. Then they pull the roof off the house, and Darcie lowers in a big, sky-colored bowl— much bigger than mine—with a plastic contraption on top of it, filled with cat food. Then another, right beside it, filled with water. Tevin picks up the roof and puts it back on top of the house, snapping it in place.

"Okay," says Ray. "That'll do it. Do you think that's enough for the whole island?" he asks Darcie.

"I would think that eight ought to do it," Darcie answers. "But we'll find out soon enough. If the food starts disappearing faster than we can keep up with it, we'll know to add another house or two."

"We need to go fill the rest of them right now," she says to Tevin. "Tomorrow morning we'll drive around the island and see if the cats found them overnight."

As they turn to walk back toward the house, I turn too, racing ahead of them before they can see me, to my home under the deck. My thoughts gallop along with my paws. The houses are not for dogs! The houses are for cats—for *feeding* cats—all over the island! My mother's quick nose will surely find one of the houses as she trudges under the moonlight, intent on the hunt. She—along with my littermates and every other hungry, weak, and starving cat on the island—will finally be fed, assured of going to sleep with her belly full, contented just as I am now, as I rest my chin on my paws and close my eyes, purring.

"Oh, my gosh, it's a Lucy!"

Darcie's exclamation interrupts my bath. I've been concentrating on that hard-to-reach spot just behind my shoulder, ignoring the sounds from the garage.

A Lucy? What does a Lucy look like? I quit my bathing and rush to the garage to see. On the floor is a trap. Darcie is kneeling beside it. Freeman stands next to her. Both have their backs to me. Inside the trap, flattened against its farthest wall, is a cat that does resemble me. She has the same sandy fur speckled with dirt-colored patches on her back, the same dark stripes that run down her legs, the same markings that I see when I bathe myself.

"Where did she come from—the yard or the lot?" Darcie asks.

"The lot," Freeman answers.

I creep forward, to get a closer look. I open my mouth to smell better.

"What's a Lucy?" Freeman asks.

I bend my ears forward.

"Oh, that's what we named our island cat," Darcie tells him. "This cat looks like Lucy. And there are a lot of Lucys down where you work. We see her relatives at that end all the time."

"So your Lucy was wild?" Freeman asks.

"Yes," Darcie says. "We're in the process of taming her right now—but it takes a long time! We brought her home in

January, and here it is summer already, and we're still working on it."

My hackles rise at Darcie's words. She's not *taming* me! I'm deciding to make friends with *her*.

"Why don't you tame all the cats, then?" Freeman continues.

"Oh, there are far too many! And most of them are too old. You have to get a feral kitten when she's really little to have much hope of making her part of the family."

"Feral?" Freeman repeats.

"That's just another word for wild," Darcie tells him.

"So do they not like humans?"

"They're just not used to being handled by humans, so they fight to get away. And of course, some humans have tried to hurt them—like your boss!"

I focus on the cat in the trap. Her eyes dart wildly. The rest of her is absolutely still. I don't recognize her smell. She is bigger than me, too big to be one of my littermates. She's about the same size as my mother, but her markings are different. Her eyes land on me, and stop moving. I hold her gaze, then slowly lower my eyelids, signaling to her that everything will be okay. I leisurely flex my paw pads, to show her how relaxed I am.

"I'll take her back to her family," Darcie continues. She drapes a towel over the cage, so that I can no longer see the other Lucy.

"Just be sure that he doesn't see you," Freeman cautions.

"I'll be careful. I took the other cat back when it was almost dark, and turned her loose right behind one of the feeders. If anyone saw me, they would have thought I was filling the dishes inside."

"Well, he's getting suspicious," Freeman warns.

"Why?"

"Because I told him we've only trapped three cats. I'm not sure he believes me. I think he expected to get a lot more."

"That's probably because the cats aren't as tempted by bait as they used to be. It's been a few days now since we put up the feeders, and they're getting enough to eat for the first time ever. They probably don't even want to *leave* the feeders right now. Did you explain that to him?"

"Yes, and he asked a lot of questions about you."

"What kind of questions?"

"Who you are, and why you're feeding the cats."

"Tell him that I'd be happy to meet him, and tell him all about it!"

"I will," Freeman answers skeptically, "but I don't think he'll talk to you. He doesn't visit anybody."

"I know—I've only laid eyes on him a couple of times when we've passed each other on the road. He doesn't even wave. And we never see him at dinners or parties. What does he do all the time?"

"Goes out in his boat—he likes to fish all by himself, and usually only in the morning or evening. During the day, he reads and watches television. He's on the computer a lot, too. He doesn't even come out in the yard very often, now that the traps are getting the cats and he doesn't have to—that's the reason I can get away with them. But he says he wants to see the next one we catch."

"See it! Why?"

"I think he wants to make sure it's dead."

"Oh, no!" Darcie says, standing up. "He's already seen one dead cat! Isn't that enough for him?"

"Guess not."

"But you can't kill any more cats, Freeman!"

"I don't want to," Freeman answers, sounding pained. "But what can I do?"

Darcie is silent for many breaths, looking at the floor. "Do you carry a radio?" she asks.

"Yes," Freeman answers. Most of the humans on the island do—workers and homeowners. The radios crackle with static on their golf carts or hang silently on their belts. They abruptly come alive with voices, the humans hailing each other.

"We do, too. We monitor Channel 7 and we answer to RayDar," Darcie tells him. "The next time you trap a cat, call me on the radio. I'll come right down and bring a syringe of tranquilizer—I keep some here in a medicine kit for the cats. You can meet me at the far edge of the lot, out of sight. We'll sedate the cat so that it looks dead. Then you can show him the cat, still in the trap. He won't want to touch it, will he?"

"I doubt it," Freeman answers. "He hates cats too much to touch one."

"Then this should work," Darcie assures him. "You can show him the cat, then drive away with the trap as though you're going to the incinerator. But bring the cat to me instead, and I'll let him recover here in the garage before I release him. Okay?"

"Okay."

"Good—thank you, Freeman." Darcie pats him on the shoulder. "Let's hope that seeing one more 'dead' cat will convince him. Now let me get this sweet little thing back to her family!"

She picks up the trap with the Lucy, and I run back under my deck.

The full light that covers the island after sunrise is becoming the best part of the day. Whether I've been out roaming in the night or asleep under my deck, as soon as I see the first hint of conch shell in the sky—a sign that the sun is about to replace the stars—I am awake and alert, hunched under the edge of my deck, waiting for Darcie.

We have a new routine.

As soon as she puts my food down, I run to eat it, right in front of her, while she coos and croons at me, repeating my name over and over, "Lucy, little Lucy Miracle, my darling little Lucy," telling me how beautiful I am, and how sweet. When the bowl is empty and my belly is full, I walk a few steps to the hedge that surrounds my shelter and start rubbing against it, leaving my scent on the scaevola. First with this side and then the other, I rub my chin and then my haunches on the hedge, sometimes chewing a little on the rough edges of bark to sharpen my teeth, leaving my saliva behind, and working up my courage to walk over to Darcie.

She sits on the edge of the concrete landing, unmoving and quiet during my display, watching.

I sink down on my knees, roll over on my back, and rock myself from side to side, waving my paws in the air as though I am swatting imaginary bugs. I steal a glance at Darcie. She is smiling. I play it up a little bit more. Another good roll and then I jump up, stand on my hind paws, stretch myself as tall as I can and bat furiously at the breeze. Oops! One back paw slips out from under me and down I go, tumbling to my stomach underneath the scaevola. I hear a muffled chuckle as I brush myself off, a bit embarrassed.

Drawn to Darcie as though to the scent of my own mother, I eventually lift my tail, elevate my ears, and walk over to her, climbing into the warmth of her lap, the softness of her ocean-colored robe. Claws in, I paw at the fabric covering her thighs, the way I used to massage my mother's belly while I nursed. Darcie caresses me, scratching my ears, my chin, my tummy. She drags her palm along the length of my back and resumes her cooing. "My little Lucy Miracle," she croons.

I answer. Just a tentative mew the first time—I have never spoken to a human before.

"Lucy!" Darcie exclaims. "You can talk!"

"Mrreow," I venture.

"What a big girl!"

"Meow..."

"Oh, my clever Miracle!"

"Mrrreoww..."

I am in full voice now—we are a duet, like the seagulls in the dawn singing of the day's first catch.

Then Darcie does something that frightens me at first, but soon becomes one of my favorite things. She picks me up and tucks me inside her robe, cupping my bottom with her hand so that all of my paws are resting on her chest, my tail is tucked underneath my tummy, and only my head is sticking out. The beat of her heart is loud, much louder than a cat's heart as it bangs through her ribs and against my hind paws.

Darcie stands up and walks us the length of the garage, through the groaning door and into the house, talking to me the entire time. "This is the television room, little Lucy," she says, "where we watch TV...this is the laundry room, where our clothes get cleaned...and here we are in the kitchen..."

Each of the rooms has its own noises—noises I remember as a jangled, nerve-wracking hubbub when I was in the cage on the sofa. The TV spits out voices that are too loud for my ears, even when I press them down fully against my head. The laundry room seems to shake, the dryer mimicking the staccato tapping of woodpeckers against a tree, the washer trembling with the slosh of water inside.

The kitchen is alive with sounds. A short, low-pitched hum, like a boat motor whizzing by: "that's the coffee pot telling us the coffee's ready," Darcie says. A screech like a distressed bird calling for help: "that's the microwave telling us the food is hot," Darcie says. A sudden whir like a helicopter landing on the island: "That's the blender mixing pancake batter." A dim clang like a scrap of metal being thrown into the garbage trailer: "That's the oven timer going off." A sudden pop like a pelican's beak hitting the water: "That means the toast is done." A groan like the garage door opening: "That's just Tevin closing the refrigerator," Darcie comforts me. The humans are moving about in the midst of this clamor, making noises of their own. Tevin is cooking, Ginger is taking dishes from the cupboard, and Ray is stopping in to ask what's for breakfast.

The first morning that Darcie takes me on this tour, I keep my head burrowed in her chest, trying to control my nervous tremors. But gradually I grow accustomed to our walk through the house—I even start to look forward to it. I begin to nudge my head out further and further from beneath her robe, as my eyes and ears take it all in.

"Good morning, Lucy," Tevin says, stopping whatever he's doing to smile at me. He tells me how pretty I am, too.

"Good morning, Lucy," Ginger says, with a friendly chuckle.

"Well, hi there, Lucy Belle," Ray drawls, always stopping to look in my eyes and pat me on top of the head. "How are you this morning?"

Each morning, Darcie walks me deeper into the house. From the kitchen to the living room, where I spent my time in the cage. From the living room to the office, where I learn that the clicking sounds I used to hear come from the computer. From the office to a sleeping room and its bathroom, then up the stairs into another sleeping room, then back through the living room and into the eating room, then past the big open windows that show the beach, then up another set of stairs and into more sleeping rooms, then back down and into another office, where a radio crackles and a telephone rings. Here Darcie squats down in the corner and shows me the box that I remember, heavy with the scent of Fred and Frisco. "This is the litter box," Darcie reminds me each morning, "the box where house kitties go to the bathroom."

Ginger walks in, carrying a scoop and a plastic bag. She bends down and begins to shovel through the gravel in the litter box. "Ginger cleans the litter box twice a day," Darcie explains, "so that it's nice and clean when the boys use it. When you start to use it, Lucy Miracle, we'll make sure that it gets cleaned more often."

"Yee-ss, we will," Ginger agrees, nodding as she opens a large container and pours more of the gravel into the litter box. I remember how much she detested my leavings on the sofa. Maybe she doesn't mind cleaning up waste here, where the humans think it's supposed to be.

I get a glimpse of Frisco only once during these morning house walks. He comes out from under the bed to sniff upwards at me, his curiosity overcoming his skittishness. Frisco is a nervous cat, jumpy at the household noises and voices the way I am—not at all like Fred, with his impervious swagger. I can tell that Frisco still doesn't like me; he arches his back, hisses, and rubs his body against Darcie. He sees me, I assume, as an intruder—and one to be jealous of, at that.

I can't really blame him. Darcie is making it clear that I am invited to become a member of the family. "Say hello to your sister," she tells Frisco. And she calls herself "Mommy" when she speaks to me. "Come on, little Lucy," she says in the mornings. "Mommy will take you back downstairs."

Fred comes to see me more often. He runs to meet us when Darcie carries me in from the garage, looking up at me with a meow that says he wants her to put me down, please, so that he can get a good sniff—but Darcie never does. "Yes,

Fred, it's Lucy, here for her morning tour," Darcie tells the big cat. But she keeps me safely inside her robe, above him—and I watch as he accompanies us for a while, meowing now and then before he goes his own way.

Sometimes, when our morning walks are over, Darcie lets Fred follow us to my deck. He lies on the landing, taking shade under the stairs, not touching or threatening me, but not ignoring me, either. He is inviting me to get to know him, and slowly I do.

Stretched out on my landing, Fred is as long as my mother and me put together, as handsome a cat as I've seen, with his glistening fur the color of night and his markings the color of ocean foam. His eyebrows are dark, except for one extra-long hair that is the color of the puffiest cloud. It juts off his face and stands proudly above and beyond the dark of him, his muscled, long, hard body, and the perfectly fearless and satisfied air that radiates off him like sun off the water. I stare at him, lonely with the desire to cuddle against him as I used to against my siblings, longing for the feel of another cat's fur, the beat of another cat's heart, the protection of a cat more confident than my beloved, struggling mother was able to be.

I begin to lie down with him, not right next to him but close enough so that we can smell each other. After a few days of this, Fred starts to stretch and roll in invitation, sprawled flat on his back or on his side to signal that he is not a threat, paws aimed toward me with their claws tucked in. The few meows he utters are soft and enticing. I feel safer and safer with every visit, until finally I stretch and roll too—and then, Fred and I touch noses in trust.

"Good kitties!" Darcie says. "That's so nice that you're making friends with Lucy, Fred!"

"Mmmmmm," purrs Fred, pleased with the praise.

But there are also days of loneliness. They start with Darcie coming to my deck, not at breakfast or dinnertime, and not just for a visit. She comes with a message.

"Little Lucy Miracle," she says, "Mommy and Daddy have to go back to Florida for a few days. You'll be just fine here with Tevin and Ginger and we'll see you when we get back. I'll miss you, little girl." She seems torn when she says goodbye, reluctant to turn and go, like an ibis standing on the shore, watching a fish disappear under a wave, but not willing to give up his dream of dinner.

Sometimes Ray—Darcie calls him "Daddy" when she speaks of him to me—comes to say goodbye, as well. "See you soon, Lucy Belle," he calls, a whisker of impatience in his voice, as though he is in a hurry.

Afterwards, there is a rush of gathering and packing, as they carry boxes and bags to load up their golf cart. The last bags to go on the cart are the boy cats in their travel carrier. Darcie and Ray put the carrier between them. The entire family is scrunched together on the front seat. I crouch under my scaevola and watch them wind their way down the drive. If they see me, they call out.

"Goodbye, Lucy Miracle," says Darcie. "See you soon, little girl."

"Next time, Lucy Belle," calls Ray.

Fred and Frisco say nothing, peering quietly from behind the firm plastic webbing that makes up the sides of their bag. It holds them in, but lets them see out.

I try to look nonchalant during these departures, as though they mean nothing to me. But more and more, I have come to dread them. The days drag on without my humans and their cats—no visits from Fred, no walks through the house, no cuddles from Darcie or Ray.

At least the turkeys come to visit. They waddle up the

driveway, gobbling for their breakfast. One bold rooster travels with them, crowing. Tevin or Ginger throws them birdseed or leftover bread and cereal. I lie on the steps outside the kitchen door and watch them eat. The male turkeys fan out their tails and strut around like peacocks, trying to attract the females. But the hens keep their heads down, jabbing their beaks at the food. They squabble with one another for the choicest bits. The rooster seems oblivious to all of them, his beak bobbing furiously. The chicks toddle behind their mothers, pecking at the ground. My tail swishes reflexively at the sight of the small birds. But I do not charge them. I stay on the step, remembering the manners my mother taught me. After they've scoured the ground for every tidbit, the turkeys go on their way, the rooster running behind them.

I visit the garage often, looking for company from Tevin while he works. I hop up onto a low metal box in the corner and meow to let him know I'm there. "Hello, little girl," he answers me and goes on working.

I develop a technique for getting into his golf cart when he's unloading deliveries, so that he will notice and talk to me. I put my front claws on the cart's floorboard and dig in hard. Then I kick off the garage floor with all my might and throw myself into the cart. Sometimes my head bumps the seat, but it is padded and hardly hurts at all. "What a big jump for such a little cat!" Tevin says.

Once, I tumble sideways from a stool that I try to reach while Tevin is sorting supplies beside it. The stool seems to rock on its own legs and throw me off. Tevin picks me up and comforts me. "You're okay, pretty little Lucy," he says, setting me down quickly. He cautions me as he gets out tools to trim the yard or clean the beach. "Be careful of this weed whacker, Lucy girl! You don't want to get tripped up in it!"

There is one machine in the garage that's particularly

frightening—but it's also fun to see it work. I've heard Ray call this machine a "relic." It is made of dark metal, dented and mottled with rust. It looks like a giant mouth, gaping open on its hinges. The machine sits on a countertop next to a tall cabinet stuffed with shovels, rakes, and saws.

Tevin carries a pile of coconuts in from the yard and sets them next to the machine. The coconuts roll around a bit, and Tevin wedges a brick against them to stop their jostling. "Time to use Old Man Simpson's coconut cracker. Stand back, Lucy!" he warns me.

I back up and watch from the middle of the garage as Tevin picks up one of the coconuts and places it on the bottom lip of the machine. He uses both hands to hold the coconut steady and keep it from rolling off. With his foot, he reaches underneath the countertop, where a thin, almost invisible wire runs from the side wall to a small bolt just inside the front leg of the counter. He nudges his toe underneath the wire and pulls on it, still holding the coconut with his hands. The machine's jaws clamp down onto the coconut, locking it in place. Tevin releases the wire and opens the cabinet. He takes out a medium sized machete and lifts it over the coconut. "Here we go, little girl!" he tells me as he raises his arm, and I duck as he chops down into the coconut with the machete.

Woody husks spatter the floor as the rounded end of the coconut falls onto the countertop. Tevin puts down the machete. His foot pulls on the wire again, and the machine's jaws spring open. Tevin removes the coconut and uses a small knife to cut a wedge from the meat inside. He takes a bite of the wedge. "Delicious!" he pronounces, and then he flips the rest of the wedge onto the floor for me. I grab it between my paws and begin to nibble as Tevin walks toward the freezer. He lifts the lid and sets the coconut inside. "The beginning of another piña colada!" he says, smiling and brushing his hands in satisfaction as the freezer door falls shut.

Tevin repeats the clamping, chopping and freezing until the pile of coconuts is gone and my belly is stuffed with the meaty fruit. Then he lifts a rake from the cabinet and heads toward the seaweed on the sand. I lie in the grass and watch him work until I get sleepy.

I also try to be in the garage when Ginger is getting ready to go feed the island cats, which is one of her jobs. For several days after the doghouses went up, Darcie went out in her golf cart to see what would happen. It turned out that the cats hopped in them immediately. "You should see the way the cats line up for their food!" Darcie told Ginger. "They are so polite about it—they sit in front of the house and wait their turns. Every once in a while one of them will get impatient and reach up and bat the tail of the cat who's inside eating. I've even seen two or three of them in a house at one time, all eating together. Yesterday I saw a mama cat carry her kitten into the feeder because it was too small to jump up—adorable!"

I try to imagine the island cats having so much food that they can wait patiently in line for a turn to eat, never needing to hunt. It's hard to do. But then I think of how full my tummy is now, and how I can have food whenever I want it. How different my life with my mother would have been if she'd had feeders to take us to!

"The cats will bat at me when I put their food in?" Ginger asks.

"Oh, no!" Darcie answers with a chuckle. "They'll run when you walk up. They don't want anything to do with humans. It will probably take a long time—and a lot of feeding—for that to change."

"They might think I'm trying to trap them!" Ginger counters.

"No, they won't," Darcie assures her. "The feeders don't

look anything like traps. The cats learned right away that they can come and go anytime they want. And besides, I told you how we caught some cats whose ears were already notched—that means they're not afraid of the traps."

"Maybe they should be," Ginger says darkly.

"Well, you have a point there," Darcie answers. "Thank God for Freeman! And the cats need you, just like they need him, Ginger," she says, coaxingly. "I can't feed them every day—I'm not always here. You are! And won't it be fun to drive around the island, see what's happening, get out in the fresh air more often?"

"I guess so," Ginger answers, unconvincingly. "But Tevin could do it, too."

"Sure he could. If you're too busy or on vacation, Tevin will feed the cats. If Freeman brings any cats in traps, Tevin will take them and set them free. But I want you to do the everyday feeding, please. I know that you'll do a great job of keeping the feeders clean," Darcie compliments her. "And the cats will appreciate that—they are very clean creatures, just like you."

"Okay," Ginger answers, and it is settled.

Each morning, she loads jugs of fresh water and a pile of freshly laundered rags on her cart. She scoops dry, fish-smelling food from one of the big shiny bags decorated with pictures of cats into a huge plastic container on the cart's back seat, and then throws the scooper on top. I leap up onto her cart's floorboard, just the way I do on Tevin's. Ginger doesn't like it. "Get down, Lucy," she warns. "I'm leaving." I rub my chin against the seat of the cart, looking up at her. "Meow?" I say, as sweetly as I know how. Ginger is unmoved. I flop down on the floorboard, curl and uncurl my tail, roll over on my back and wave a paw in the air.

"Oh, okay!" Ginger says, her eyes crinkling with the

smallest trace of a smile. She tosses a handful of the food onto the garage floor. I get down.

The smell of food sometimes attracts another island cat. When I see one slinking toward the garage door, I lift my tail, lower my ears and stare the cat down until he leaves. This is my territory.

When Darcie and Ray return from their times away, I come running toward the garage from wherever I am as soon as I hear their cart—or onto the beach if they come by boat. They unload the boys, and then Darcie comes to see me, picking me up the instant I get close enough. "Oh hello, my little darling, my little Lucy," she purrs at me. "Mommy missed you so, so much." She holds me up in front of her face, one hand on my rear, the other hand holding me firmly under my front legs, and looks deep into my eyes, slowly blinking her own eyes in the way that says, "I love and trust you," in cat language.

Ray usually comes with her. "Are you giving Lucy fuzzy wuzzy eyes?" he teases.

"Yes," Darcie answers, not taking her gaze from me as she asks, "Did you miss us?"

Oh yes, I want to say, oh yes. Then she kisses me, on my nose, on my cheeks, beside my mouth, even on my ear with the jagged, missing tip…and my purring starts like the growl of a distant storm, uncontrollable.

Sometimes Fred comes with her. I'm not sure whether he has missed me or is a little bit jealous, or both, but either way, there he is—Darcie approves of the visits. "Here's your Bahamian sister, Fred," she'll say. "I bet she missed you, big boy!"

She watches as Fred and I touch noses, then takes him into the house. Fred never protests, but I begin to wish that he could stay outside and roam with me all day, anywhere we want to go. Instead, he comes and goes from inside the house to

the boy cats' outdoor patio and back, while I lie down outside
the bougainvillea hedge that surrounds the patio and listen. I
hear the boys' bells first thing in the morning, as they wander
and play. I hear their meows as they talk to each other and
their good-humored growls as they wrestle. "Meow?" Fred will
say, inviting Frisco to play. "Meeeoww," Frisco answers in his
whinier, uncertain way. "Meow!!!" Fred responds, decisively.
And then they are at it, tussling and teasing, their throats
humming and their collars ringing. I contemplate ignoring
the bougainvillea briars and worming my way underneath the
hedge. I think that Fred would welcome me onto their patio,
but I am not sure about Frisco. So I just eavesdrop on their
sounds.

More and more often now, the days seem to end too
soon for me, with the final closing of the garage door after
my dinner. By that time the boys have been locked inside the
house for the night. Darcie picks up my empty bowl and
says, "Goodnight, see you in the morning, Lucy girl. Have a
good sleep." Then she is gone.

I'm not ready for sleep, though. This is the best time for
me to prowl, under cover of the dusk, and then the dark. But
before I go off on my ramble, I walk to the back yard, just
off the beach, and sit on the damp grass, watching the house
through the windows. What I used to think was the worst part
of being a housecat—staying inside—begins to look like a
pleasure. There's Fred, curled up on the couch, snoozing. There's
Frisco, sitting in Darcie's lap or following her around, rubbing
up against her legs when they are alone, or scampering up the
stairs to his sleeping room if the house gets too noisy for such
a skittish cat.

And oh, the noise of the humans! When friends are
staying in the house, or there are visitors from the island, they
cluster around the eating table while Tevin and Ginger load it

with food, enough food to feed all the cats on the island for days and days. Before they start eating, everybody around the table holds hands, a ring of people closing their eyes and dipping their chins down as though going for a water bowl. Then their forks go back and forth, back and forth, from the plates to their mouths. Tevin and Ginger take those plates away and bring clean plates and more food, while the humans talk and laugh and even pet each other. During dinner, Ray likes to put his arm around Darcie's back, stroking her hair, pulling on it as though it were a cat tail. Some of the others touch, too, putting their arms around each other, holding hands, even kissing; and when everyone finally gets up from the table, there is a great deal of hugging and kissing all around the room.

Tevin and Ginger say goodnight to everyone and go back to their cottages. The visitors leave the house through the garage door and get into their golf carts, heading back to their own houses on the island. Or, if there are people who have arrived with suitcases, they go upstairs to sleep. Darcie and Ray often bring friends to the island after their times away. The friends spend a lot of time outdoors while they are here, and don't usually stay very long. Their faces are always changing, new people coming to visit.

One lazy evening after I've eaten dinner and Darcie and the visitors have all gone inside, I sprawl out on my landing, alternating between bathing and dozing. My stomach feels too full to start my evening walk. When a plodding sound begins in the side yard, I sit up. The sound gets closer and quickens. It is the sound of footsteps—quiet, unfamiliar footsteps. I duck beneath the scaevola hedge, where I am hidden but can still see out. Dark boots are heading toward the house—thick, heavy boots with toes that look too big, nothing like the open flip-flops and flimsy moccasins that most humans wear. The boots draw closer and closer to the

hedge, until they are almost touching it. My whiskers begin
to tremble. Just as I am about to make a run for the deck, the
boots turn away from me and sidle down the hedge, shuffling
now, toward the far entrance to the garage.

I move stealthily along the ground, under cover of the
hedge, dragging my stomach in the dirt, a step or two behind
the boots. They stop as they reach the end of the hedge. I am
so close that I can hear the human breathe. There is the faint
creak of bones above me, as though he is turning his neck to
look around. The boots move again, abruptly, startling me. I
gasp for air. The boots trudge toward the garage, out of my
sight. I slant my ears in their direction, and again I hear the
plodding, not as dull this time, against the concrete floor of
the garage. The plodding drifts away from me, out of range
of my hearing. I emerge from underneath the hedge and race
along the wall to the other end of the garage. I get low again
and steal toward the entrance. I plaster my whiskers back
against my cheeks and poke my face around the wall, just far
enough to see into the garage.

The palest, thinnest human I have ever seen is edging
along the wall of the garage, past the bathroom and down the
length of the shelves that hold snorkel gear, rafts, and beach
toys. Dark socks jut out of his boots, and above them are legs
the color of the puffy clouds that dot the sky on a rainless day.
Curly hairs coil out from his pasty skin like cockroach legs.
He wears baggy shorts, scrunched in at the waist by a belt, and
a long-sleeved shirt. His face is as pale as his legs, as though
it has never been touched by the sun. His lips are thin and
turn downward. His cheekbones push against his flesh. His
eyes are covered with large dark glasses, and a cap and visor
obscure his forehead. Below the cap, the back of his head is
bald.

After every few steps, the man stops and looks around: a

quick glance toward the groaning door, then down the driveway. When he looks toward the beach, through the entrance where I am hiding, I pull my nose back. The creak of his neck is louder than it was outside.

He pauses at the pile of cat food bags. At his feet are the jugs that Ginger uses to haul water and the plastic container that she puts the food in. The scooper lies in the middle of the container, lonely and stark. The man squats down, his pale thighs settling onto his calves. He picks up the scooper and turns it over in his hands. He puts it back in the container and stands up, the bones of his knees scraping. He raises himself to his toes, the tips of his shoes flattening against the floor. The visor of his cap hangs over the edge of the top bag of cat food as he examines it. One finger prods at the bag. There's the rustle of dry food inside, and he jerks his hand back.

He takes another look around, shuffles farther along. He comes to a wooden cabinet that reaches high up the wall and fumbles with the rusty latch that holds it shut. There is a rasp of metal as the latch gives way, and he stiffens, then looks around again. Slowly and noiselessly, he swings open the cabinet's double doors. His skinny fingers begin to rummage inside. They find the spare, empty water bottles that go in the doghouses where the cats eat. He picks one up, turns it upside down, and inspects the bowl that it's screwed onto. He sniffs at the bowl, then puts it back. Next, he picks up a similar contraption that holds the food. It is larger than the water bottle, and the hole at the bottom is wider so that the food can easily fall out of the container into the bowl below. He unscrews the food container from the bowl, holding one piece in each hand. He turns the container upside down and smells it. He holds it up in front of his face, toward the light, scrutinizing it. He screws the top back onto the bowl, slowly and carefully. Then he closes the cabinet door and pounds at the latch with the heel of his hand, making a slight slapping sound, until it closes.

He tiptoes toward the tool cabinet, running his hand along the countertop below it. The thick, big toe of his boot rams against the cabinet leg, and he trips on the thin strand of wire that Tevin uses to run the coconut cracker. Trying to stop himself from falling, the man pitches forward and grabs on to the old rusted machine, just as its jaws begin to move. And then, as fast as a bolt of lightning, Old Man Simpson's coconut cracker locks its jaws onto the man's finger. I hear the crunch of bone breaking. The man bites his lip, swallowing a yelp. A moan gurgles and dies in his throat.

The man thrashes, trying to free his finger. His eyes dart around like a trapped cat's, looking for escape. He uses his free hand to try to pry the jaws of the machine apart, gripping and straining, but the machine doesn't budge. He stops wrestling and studies his finger, lips clenched. Then he takes his free hand and runs it along the edges of the machine, over its top, down its sides and under its bottom, searching for something. The hand comes up empty. Next, he runs his hand along the countertop, beneath it, along its edges and back into the corners where it meets the wall, twisting his body over the trapped finger. Nothing. Finally, the man goes still, feet planted beneath the machine, head bent over it. A long sigh whooshes out of him like air from the compressor that inflates the bicycle tires. And then he is utterly quiet, unmoving.

A drop of thick, dark liquid oozes over the jaw of the coconut cracker, slides down the edge of the countertop and splatters on the floor like a rotten sea grape bursting open on the ground. Blood. The man appears not to notice as another drop unhurriedly worms its way down and splashes on the pale cement. Just behind it, another trickle, another splatter. I watch, transfixed, as the drops continue and cluster together until they look like an entire bunch of over ripened sea grapes squashed upon the floor.

The man stays so still that I wonder whether he has begun to doze, or perhaps even passed out with pain. I work up my courage and creep into the garage. I jump onto an old crate in the corner so that I can see him better. It totters a bit, but the man doesn't move. Satisfied that he is still, I hop down and try to walk noiselessly behind him, my claws scrunched all the way in so that only my pads hit the floor. I pass his ankles and take a few more cautious steps. When I am almost at the tool cabinet, I turn to look up at his face. The man's head jerks up, his eyes fly open, and he looks straight at me. "Scat!" he yelps.

Shocked, I jump back and away from him, but I am up against the tool cabinet now, and there is nowhere for me to go. The wire stretches out in front of me. I try to jump over it, flinging myself into the air, but my leap isn't high enough and I fall, hard, onto the wire. It digs into my flesh. I let out a low squeal, and at the same time I hear the hinges of the old machine as its jaws crank open. The man jerks his finger free. It hangs crookedly, blood-smeared and smelling of salt. He cradles the mangled finger in his other hand, studying me as I look up at him, trapped against the cabinet and too stunned to make a run for it. In his eyes I see pain and confusion. Suddenly, he sprints away. His motion is so abrupt that only my whiskers stir, instinctively drawing back from the breeze of his body as he dashes by me and out the beach entrance, turning the corner toward the side yard.

Just then, Ray's golf cart pulls up the driveway and into the garage. He clicks the key in the cart, silencing its electric motor. Its lights die out. Ray stares briefly at the corner where the cat food is piled. He gets out of the cart and walks toward the beach, stopping on the sidewalk to peer at the side yard.

Then he shakes his head, a brisk side-to-side movement, and turns back into the garage. The door is groaning open.

"Hi, there!" Darcie calls to Ray. "You're just in time for dinner! How'd the meeting go?"

"Pretty well," Ray answers. "We've pretty much decided to build a new seawall along the airport, if we can find a reasonable contractor. Was somebody just in the garage?"

"I don't know," Darcie answers. "I think everyone's inside. Maybe Tevin was out here to get something from the freezer. Why?"

"Because I swear I saw someone in the garage as I pulled up. And then he disappeared around the corner. But I just looked in the yard, and it's empty."

"What did he look like?" Darcie asks.

"He was tall and thin—and really pale," Ray answers. "This might be crazy, but I think I know who it was, even though I've only seen him a couple of times." Then he says the name that makes my whiskers bristle. "Uberan." Of course! The cat hater that screamed "Scat!" at my mother. Why didn't I recognize him? Maybe because I never expected to see him here in our garage, rather than hidden behind his own wire barricade, plotting our demise.

"Oh, my gosh!" says Darcie. "Freeman was going to ask him to come down and talk to me."

"Well, if that's who it was, he wasn't here to talk to anybody—not running out of the garage like that. But I don't know, maybe I imagined it. I was still thinking about what would make the best seawall, concrete or steel…" Ray's voice trails off as he and Darcie head toward the door and disappear inside.

The next day, as the sun is growing weak, I lie on the sidewalk watching Darcie and Ray on the beach with their friends. Each of them holds a coconut with a straw and a tiny paper umbrella protruding from a hole in its top. They sip from the straws as they tell stories of the day's adventures and talk about what they'll do tomorrow: Snorkeling? Diving? Shelling on the flats? Dishes clatter and cooking smells come from the house—the humans' dinner being prepared. I begin to salivate in anticipation of my own supper. I am wondering what flavor it will be tonight—salmon? tuna? trout?—when Freeman pulls into the garage. Two traps covered with towels are on the back of his golf cart. He takes them off the cart and sets them in the far corner. Then he walks outside. "Miss Darcie?" he calls.

Both Darcie and Ray come to the garage. The friends stay in their beach chairs.

"I have more cats," Freeman says.

Darcie hesitates. "Alive—or dead?" she asks.

"Alive!" Freeman answers gleefully.

"Wonderful! But you didn't radio me. How'd you get away with them?" Darcie asks. "I thought he wanted to see the next cat."

"He did. But he's gone to Bimini for the night and won't be home until tomorrow. I didn't want to hold them in the traps for that long. I thought about setting them free, but you asked me to bring you all the cats."

"That's fine," Darcie says. "It's best not to release them near Uberan's property, where they might wander right back into the yard."

"Is there any chance your boss was down here last night?" Ray asks. "I thought I saw somebody who looked like him in our garage."

"Well…could have been, I guess. He pretty much only leaves the house at night. But I don't know why he would come here."

"Do you think he might have come to talk to me? Did you ask him whether I could speak with him?" Darcie asks.

"No, I'm afraid not," Freeman confesses. "I was going to. But when I mentioned the cats, he stopped me right away and asked whether we had any more dead ones."

"Oh. When was that?" Darcie asks.

"Yesterday. I had to tell him no, of course. And he didn't like it one little bit. So I thought hard all morning while I was raking the turtle grass off the beach, and I came up with a plan of my own," Freeman says proudly.

"What's that?" Darcie asks.

"Well, you know Mosey, the guy who works at the incinerator?"

"Yes," Darcie and Ray say at the same time.

"He works after hours with me…comes down to the house and cleans out the fire pit, brings gas for the grill, stuff like that. We're pretty good buddies—and the boss likes him, too. They talk sometimes while Mosey's working."

"*They* talk?" Darcie asks. "I thought he didn't talk to anybody. What's different about Mosey?"

"Well for one thing, he doesn't get there until well after five o'clock—and by then, the boss has had a drink or two. And Mosey likes to talk about fishing. He tells him the best spots to go, and when—that kind of thing."

"Okay—so how does Mosey fit into your plan?" Ray asks.

"Well, I took a little towel today and rolled it up tight, so that it was about this long," Freeman says, holding out his hands, one on each side of his chest. "Then I took an old dust mop—you know, the fuzzy kind with the yellow nappy stuff all over it? I wrapped the fuzz around the towel—even made a tail that sorta hung off from the whole thing. Then I put it in a plastic garbage bag and tied the bag kinda loose around it."

"So that it looked like a dead cat in a bag?" Darcie asks.

"All right, all right!" Freeman answers with a smile. "I took it down to Mosey at the incinerator, and told him we needed to burn it up right away. I said if we didn't, it would start stinking and maybe draw flies. Mosey didn't much want to handle it—I'd kinda figured on that—but it's the fastest I ever saw him move. He grabbed that bag out of my hands and threw it into the fire so quick, you woulda thought it was a barracuda on his fishing line!" Freeman chuckles. "Tomorrow, when the boss gets back, I'll tell him we got us a dead cat and he's already burnt up!"

"And then Mosey will confirm your story, of course, when he comes to work," Darcie says.

"That's what I'm figuring on."

"That was really smart of you, Freeman," Darcie tells him. "Really smart. Maybe it'll satisfy him for a while. And just in time, too—we need to go back to Florida. I won't be gone long, though—a few days or so."

"And I'm going to tell Tevin and Ginger to be on the lookout for anybody coming or going around here," Ray says. "It bugs me that your boss might have been in the garage—because if it was him, he obviously didn't want to be seen. I know you have a lot to do already, Freeman, but if you have any suspicions that he's heading this way, let Tevin and Ginger know, would you? I'd really like to find out what he'd be doing around here."

I can't sit still on the sidewalk any longer. I march into the garage, meowing as loudly as I can. Ray, Darcie, and Freeman all look at me.

"Oh my goodness—Lucy!" Darcie exclaims. "What a big girl you're being, strutting right into the garage like this! Do you want to talk with us?"

"So that's Lucy!" Freeman says, eyeing me. "She's a pretty one."

I ignore the compliment and walk over to the cat food bags and stretch myself up on my hind legs, leaning against the pile. I begin to claw at the bags, meowing and looking from the bags to the humans and back again.

"Oh, Lucy girl," Darcie says. "I get it—it's almost dinnertime, and you're hungry. I'll get your food in just a few minutes. But leave those bags alone, please—you don't want to tear a hole in them." She strides toward me. I evade her, marching over to the cabinet where the spare containers and bowls are kept. I rub up against it, meowing earnestly and looking first at Darcie, then at Ray.

"Come on over here, Lucy," Ray beckons. "If you want a good rub, I'll give you one."

I meow again and walk to the empty container with the scooper in it. I hop inside and bat the scooper around with my paw. I look up at them. They are all smiling. "I've never seen her play like this before!" Darcie says.

Frustrated, I jump out of the container and walk toward the tool cabinet. I look up at the countertop holding the machine. I lift my paw to touch the wire, but Ray yells, "Lucy, don't!" startling me away. "We should put a flag or something on that wire, if we're going to keep that old relic forever," he tells Darcie.

Still determined, I walk back to the floor just beneath the machine and squat down on my haunches beside the dried drops of blood. "Mrreow," I say.

"I don't know why we still have it," answers Darcie, looking at Ray. "Can't Tevin crack coconuts without that rusty old contraption cluttering up the garage?"

"*Mrreow!*" I say.

"I'm sure he could, but it's fun to have an antique like that around, don't you think?" Ray asks.

"MRREEEOW!" I screech.

"*What*, Lucy?" Ray asks, he and Darcie finally looking at me.

I paw at the floor, my claws scraping the cement. Ray walks over to me and squats down to inspect the dark splotches. Darcie follows him.

"What is that?" she asks.

"It looks like dried blood," Ray tells her.

"I *knew* that machine was dangerous!" Darcie says. "I hope Tevin didn't hurt himself."

"Tevin would have told us," Ray replies. "I'm wondering just whose blood this is. Maybe it's Uberan's."

"What in the world would he be doing with our coconut machine?" Darcie asks.

"No telling with that man," Freeman says. "If he was here, he was probably snooping around at anything he could get his hands on."

"If he was here snooping, it's time to have a few words with him, whether he wants to talk or not," Ray says, tensely.

Satisfied, I saunter from the garage and lie on my tummy just outside the entrance, watching and listening until the humans say their good-byes. They seem to have forgotten all about me.

Freeman drives away. Darcie goes into the house. Ray strolls back to the friends on the beach and picks up his coconut.

I walk over to the traps Freeman left in the garage and nose at the towel that covers the closest one, not wanting to claw it off completely and scare the cat inside. I nudge the towel toward the top of the trap until I get it up high enough to see him. He's lying down, right in the middle of the wire floor—a cat that's bigger than my mother and dusky all over. An overturned bowl lies beside him, empty. He hisses at me. I pull my face away, and his towel drops back down.

As I start nosing the towel on the next trap, my heart

jumps a bit. I see sandy fur like my own, and similar markings. I spring up onto the roof of the cage. My claws catch the edge of the towel and I fall off, dragging the towel with me. But now I can see the whole cat. A stripe like the night sky runs up her belly and winds its way to her head, which is dark all over. Her ears are flattened against her head. She stares at me, apprehensive and questioning. I return her gaze, steady and reassuring, lowering my eyelids to let her know that she can trust me. Her ears lift. I meow softly, desperately wanting to let her know that before evening she'll be back on her own territory. She settles onto her paws and meows back a tentative thank you, mildly comforted. I grab the towel in my teeth, try to throw it back up on top of the cage, but it is too heavy. I nose it up against the bars as best I can and return to my deck to wait for dinner.

I am on edge and on the lookout while Darcie and Ray and the boy cats are away. I stay close to the house and shrubbery during the day, so that I can take cover quickly. My sleep is fitful, even in the darkest, safest corner beneath my deck. Nightmares plague me. I wake myself, twitching, my paws clawing at the air as though I were actually running. But the man who makes my whiskers bristle doesn't come back; I don't see or smell him.

When I hear the motorboat that announces the return of Darcie, Ray and the boys, I race out from underneath my deck and onto the sidewalk that leads to the beach. An entire litter of female humans piles off the boat, throwing their suitcases onto the sand, talking and laughing. Only Darcie is with them—no Ray and no boys.

"Oh my gosh, what a paradise!" a female exclaims.

"Look at the color of that water. It's positively turquoise," says another.

"Look at the hammock. It's all mine!" declares the female in the middle, pointing and laughing.

They are excited, cooing like seagulls over a handful of bread thrown on the sand, as they go into the garage and through the creaking door, Tevin and Ginger toting their suitcases after them. Soon they are scampering back to the beach in their bathing suits, stopping on the garage side of my deck to throw off their shoes. I follow behind them, out of sight, slinking low beneath the scaevola. They drag the lounge chairs that dot the beach closer together, into a row. They throw towels on the chairs and sit down on them, stretching their bodies out like cats—all except Darcie. She comes for me, calling.

"Lucy Miracle, where are you? Do you want to come to the beach and meet my girlfriends? They want to meet you!" I poke my head out from underneath the scaevola, and Darcie picks me up.

"Well, that's so nice that you want to join us, little Lucy," she says, petting me and kissing my head. She carries me down to the line of chairs, and the girlfriends start clamoring for me, sounding even more like those seagulls. They all want to get their hands on me!

"Oh, look how beautiful she is! So dainty, and it looks like she has eyeliner on! Let me have the little darling," says a girlfriend called Scarlett.

"No, I get her first," answers a girlfriend called Angelina. Her voice is sweet but sharp.

"I think she wants to come to *me*," says the girlfriend called Lorraine, in that cooing voice that Darcie and Ray often use.

Darcie holds me high and close against her chest until she says, "I think Scarlett had first dibs." She hands me off, like a just-picked coconut, to the girlfriend called Scarlett.

I shudder a bit as this new human wraps her hands around me, but my nervous trembling quickly turns into quivers of pleasure. Scarlett holds me tightly against her chest, my chin resting on her shoulder, her chin against my head. "Well, Lucy, you are just the most precious little thing," she says, stroking my back. "Such a tiny little thing."

I fall asleep purring, waking up when I am passed from Scarlett to the girlfriend called Lorraine. Lorraine's touch is as light as Scarlett's, a gentle stroke, but she also uses her fingernails to scratch me lightly. "My little girl Lynette would just love to have you," says Lorraine, purring at me. "You're one of the prettiest little kitties I've ever seen." She lays me in her lap, petting me and petting me, until I fall asleep again, purring.

I'm awakened by the girlfriend called Angelina. "You've had enough of a turn, give her to me," she says in that voice that's nice but has an edge to it, as though she really means what she's saying.

"Oh, okay, if I have to," responds Lorraine, and just like one of those coconut drinks, off I go again. This time, I don't fall asleep; I have had my fill of naps. I stay awake to feel every caress, up and down my back, around my ears, under my chin.

I don't purr while Elli holds me. She doesn't seem to know where to put me, resting me on her shoulder, then her lap, then her stomach, holding and moving me unsteadily, so that my legs hang lower on one side than the other. Will she drop me? I take charge and begin to climb the soft rungs on the back of her chair, but the rungs are more slippery than they look. I lose my footing and a dangling paw swishes through Elli's hair. She laughs and runs her hand across her head. "What are you doing, giving me a new hairdo?" she asks.

I pull up my paw and keep climbing until I reach the highest part of the chair, several rungs above her head. She can't see me back here. "Lucy!" she calls. I gently bat her hair with my paw. "*Lucy!*" she exclaims. I bat her hair on the other side. Elli reaches up behind her, trying to find my paw. I pull it back and under my stomach. I am having fun now!

Elli pulls her back away from the chair so that she can twist around to look at me. "What *are* you doing that for?" she asks. I lower my eyelids at her. Then I hop down onto the towel next to her thighs, and from there onto her lap. I settle myself firmly on top of her legs. "Okay, then, but you be a good girl!" Elli admonishes. I rest my head on my paws. Elli pats my back. My eyes get heavy and I sleep again.

The next several days are like this: utterly delicious, like the warmest dream about being back with my mother and my littermates. The girlfriends take up their positions on the beach and call for me. I swagger down the sand, taking my time. I pause beside a tree stump along the beach and decide to use it as a vantage point for choosing which girlfriend to grace with a visit. I spring off my hind legs, aiming for the top of the stump, but don't get close enough to sink a claw. I sprawl back on the beach, my chin plowing a small ditch in the sand. I stand up and shake myself off. Sand flies from my whiskers. I sneeze. "How adorable!" a girlfriend says.

"I think that tree stump is a little bit high for you, Lucy!" another calls out to me.

Of course it's high, I think—that's why I missed! But I know I can make it, and besides, I want to impress the girlfriends. This time, I move further back and crouch down harder to get more spring as I hurl myself into the air. My front paws sink into the edge of the stump and I haul myself up to the level surface at its top. I bump into a glass that is resting there, knocking it over and sending ice cubes rattling along the wood. The girlfriends giggle. "Lucy, your aim needs a little work!" calls the girlfriend called Isabel.

Embarrassed, I turn my back to them and start to bathe, as though I meant to get rid of the glass and make space for my grooming. I stretch a hind paw out as far as it will reach, taking up as much of the stump as I can while I lower my head to wash that leg. I even lick an ice cube, as though using it to help me clean myself.

"Oh, don't tease her—she's just learning how to maneuver," Darcie admonishes the girlfriends. "She's only a bitty thing, after all!" Darcie walks over and picks me up, interrupting my bath. She lifts me to her face and we touch noses. Then she sets me gently back on the stump, picking up the fallen glass in the process. The girlfriends resume their competitive clamor.

I swivel my head to study the row of chairs, consider their invitations. "Come here, Lucy," calls the light-haired one, patting her lap.

"Lucy, kitty, kitty," says another, holding out her hand.

"Oh, come to me first," invites a girlfriend at the end of the row, patting the empty space beside her on the chair.

I select a girlfriend who smells like coconut water mixed with banana, amble over and hop up. She pets me for a bit and then carries me to the girlfriend next to her. They pass me from hand to hand, chair to chair, up and down the line, and I go limp with acceptance and pleasure as they take turns caressing me, until the sun sinks low over the water.

What would Frisco think? I wonder. He hides from stranger humans—he would never let himself be passed around like a coconut. Would he think I'm being foolish, so easily seduced by visitors? Or would he be envious to watch me getting so much affection? And what about Fred? I bet he would be right here with me, vying for attention. Fred loves to throw himself up against humans, slamming his side into their legs as he arches his back and thrusts his tail high into the air, saying, "Notice me. Talk to me. Pet me."

I practice part of his technique. I nose a girlfriend, then

meow at her, raise my tail and turn away, still meowing as I take a few steps, looking back over my shoulder. Elli is the first to understand. She follows me down the beach, then returns and tells the others, "Lucy likes to take people for walks!"

"Really?" Lorraine asks. "How far did you go?"

"She led me all the way to the rocks on the point," Elli replies.

"Wow, that's pretty far for a little cat with such short legs!" Scarlett says. Her tone is kindly, but I am annoyed—even more so when Isabel chimes in.

"I didn't know cats went for walks with people!" she says.

"I've certainly never had a cat take me for a walk," says another girlfriend. "I thought only dogs did that."

"Well, if a cat came up to you and meowed, would you know to follow her?" asks Angelina.

And these people think they are taming *me*?

The next time I walk Elli, I decide to show her how big I am. She is several strides behind me when I come upon a snake, its tail wriggling next to a bougainvillea bush. At first, I think it's an extra-large gecko—snakes are such a rarity on the island. But as I sneak up on it, the lizard keeps getting longer and longer, until I realize what it is. I remember my kittenhood fear of snakes. I also remember my mother's special skills at catching them: creeping up behind them, lunging rapidly, and grasping them just behind the head so that they couldn't whip around and sink their fangs into her. I summon my courage, steal behind the snake and hit it with all my teeth in exactly the right spot, clamping my jaws shut, tight on its slimy throat. I shake it until it stops squirming. Triumphantly, I carry my trophy to Elli. I drop the snake at her feet and nose at it to show it off, purring and proud.

"Oh, Lucy," Elli says, a tone in her voice that surprises

me—like the sound of a lawn mower sputtering into silence. "You got a snake." She looks down, not squatting to touch or smell my catch, not praising me or patting me, but scrunching up her nose as though I'd shown her something inedible and nasty, like a shred of mildewed plastic or a piece of barnacle-covered rope. When our mother brought my siblings and me a snake, we mewed in admiration at the special feast. But Elli turns back to the beach; I follow as she tells the litter of women about my kill with her nose still crinkled in distaste.

"What do you feed that cat, soybeans?" asks Angelina.

"No," says Darcie, laughing gently. "That's not why she's a hunter. It's because of her feral childhood—remember, she was starving and had to hunt to survive. I *would* give her veggie food, though, if I were single, but Ray thinks that's going too far. So we compromise on cat food made from fish."

"How long have you been a vegetarian?" Scarlett asks.

"So long that I have to stop and remember how old I am," Darcie answers, closing her eyes for a moment. "I guess it's been over thirty years now."

"You're a vegetarian because you grew up on a farm?" asks the girlfriend named Isabel.

"Yes, on a hobby farm. We had lots of different animals: horses, sheep, cows. We fed the baby cows milk out of buckets with big rubber nipples on them. We gave them names, scratched their ears, played with them in the pasture, watched them grow up and then, watched them go away. Sometime in there, I realized what "beef" was, and that was it for me and meat."

"You don't even eat fish, do you?" asks Scarlett.

Darcie shakes her head no.

"How about dairy, eggs, or any animal products?" asks Angelina.

Darcie shakes her head no.

"Do you ever miss it?"

"Oh no," says Darcie. "Sentient creatures are not food to me; I can't conceive of them that way. They all think and feel—and suffer. Besides, how can you hold, pet, feed and love one animal, and then turn around and eat another one for dinner?"

None of the girlfriends answer.

That night, at dusk, after Darcie has gone inside, I scamper up a palm tree in the back yard, high enough to be shielded by its fronds but close enough to see into the windows of the house.

I watch as the girlfriends gather around the eating table, chattering. Tevin and Ginger come and go, serving food and clearing dishes. Out of habit, I look for the boys. But there is no Fred rubbing up against the girlfriends' legs or lying on a chair. There is no Frisco darting up the stairs to escape the commotion. For the first time since Darcie arrived, I miss them.

The cat-less scene is lit by the glow of a lamp that dangles from the ceiling. The lamp is shaped like a bunch of flowers hanging upside down, as though the humans are try- ing to bring the outdoors in. The light casts dainty shadows on the girlfriends' faces. At the far ends of the table, candles flicker. Their flames bend in the breeze, like human fingers beckoning.

The girlfriends clustered around that table, I realize, are freer than any island cat could ever hope to be. Humans can wander my island and enjoy its beaches and grasses and trees. They can swim in the ocean that surrounds it. They can get in their boats and planes and leave the island, off to the place called Florida or wherever else they go. They can come back whenever they please. And yet with all that freedom, this is what the humans choose to do: live inside houses, with friends and family and food.

I claw my way down the tree trunk, head first, and leap to the ground, then canter across the narrow stretch of spongy grass between the tree and the house. The windowsill that runs the length of the eating room is half a human high, a huge jump for me. But I am resolute. I study the windowsill, sizing it up, then walk back a little to give myself a running start, and hurl myself forward through the air. My paws barely hit the smooth rim of the windowsill, and I cannot hold on. I plunge into the plot of flowers just below it. I shake myself off and walk back out onto the grass. This time, I start further out and run harder. I land on the windowsill with all of my feet, turn myself sideways as fast as I can, and start prancing up and down its length, arching my back to make myself taller, feeling big and proud of myself, waiting for the girlfriends to notice me.

They don't. They keep on talking. They are wrapped up in one another like a litter of newborns, clumped so closely together that you can barely tell where one kitten ends and another begins.

So I start talking, too. I meow as loudly as I can, still pacing from one end of the windowsill to the other, my mouth toward the shield of glass that separates me from the indoors.

"M r r r e o w w w . . . . M r r e o w w w . . . . M R R e o w w . . . . MRRRREEOWWWWW...," I scream until, at last, Scarlett points to the window.

"Look!" Scarlett exclaims. "There's Lucy!"

"Oh, my gosh, how cute!" says Angelina. "Do you think she wants to come in?"

"MRRREOWWWW!"

Darcie is sitting with her back toward the window and has to swivel around to see me.

"MRRREEOWWWW!" I tell her, and then softer, more pleadingly, now that I have her attention: "Mrreeoww?"

"Well, of course, Lucy," she answers me. "We would be delighted to have you come in."

Darcie gets up and walks out of my sight. She is headed toward the television room, so I bound down from the windowsill, not even stopping to think about how big a jump it is, barely noticing the thump of my paws on the concrete below, and run to the door there. It opens for me just as I reach it. I slow down, pause to inhale the human smells, lift my front paw, and for the first time ever, walk into the house all by myself.

The girlfriends call to me like a flock of birds calling home a fledgling.

"Welcome, Lucy!"

"Hello, Lucy Miracle. Nice to have you with us!"

"Well, well, I think somebody has decided she wants to be a housecat," Isabel says.

I want to run to them, leap into their laps, and give myself over to their stroking and cuddling, as I do on the beach. But there is something I must do first, something that is essential to becoming a housecat.

I turn and walk, decisively, toward where I know I must go. Darcie follows me. "Where are you going, little Lucy?" she asks, her voice lilting upwards with curiosity.

I don't answer; I just keep walking toward the room with the box that the boys use. "Oh!" exclaims Darcie, when we are almost there.

I catch the scent of the boys as I enter the room; it is faint but unmistakable, rising out of the box. In the boys' absence, the litter looks fresh and unused. I raise my paws and hop inside. Scratch, scratch: I dig a shallow hole right in the middle of the litter and squat down over it. I let loose as much urine as I can muster and then step away from the hole.

Scratch, scratch: I cover the puddle with dirt, stopping now and again to sniff at my work. When I am sure that all of my waste is buried, I hop out and look up at Darcie.

She lifts me into her arms and showers kisses on me like raindrops, all over my head, my ears, my eyes, my nose, my chin. "Oh, my darling little Lucy Miracle," Darcie says, "my good, good girl. Good, clever girl. Such a big girl!"

I purr at the words "clever" and "big girl" and keep on purring, as the girlfriends pass me from lap to lap, right up through the moment when Darcie carries me to her sleeping room and into bed with her, nestling me next to her loud human heart in a pile of warm, soft cloths. Reflexively, my paws begin to massage the bedding.

"Mommy," I think, dreamily. My purr deepens into a rumble. As I dig further and further into the bedding, I feel human skin beneath it. I am kneading, kneading Mommy as sleep creeps up on me, and I am gone.

CHAPTER FIVE

Family Cat

Frisco doesn't want me here. He tells me so the moment he returns with Ray and Fred.

The girlfriends have gone, and the house is quiet. I am in the laundry room—my new eating place—nuzzling a bowl of fresh warm food, when the garage door creaks open and I hear them come in. Fred and Frisco pick up my scent before the door has even swung shut, and they follow it to the laundry room, where I take cover beside the washer. Frisco slinks toward me, fur puffed out like the duster that leans in the corner, ears back, tail and nose twitching. He stops a few whiskers away from me, arches his back, and hisses in my face, long, low and mean.

I pull my ears in but lower my eyes, telling the dark boy cat that I do not wish to fight. I sit as still as a cornered rat staring at the open beak of a heron, my heart beating furiously. Frisco stops hissing, sniffs at me, hisses again, then turns and walks slowly out of the room, tail erect. He hasn't hurt me, hasn't bared his teeth or claws, or even aimed his tail as though to spray me, but his message is clear: he wants me out of his territory.

Fred stands by the door watching this encounter. After Frisco leaves, Fred stares at me, then saunters over, taking his time, his tail swishing like a leaf in a light breeze. I stay still, trembling a little, as he lowers his head and inhales my odors, starting at my skull and moving along my body to my tail—a thorough sniff, telling him that I have indeed moved into the house. On my body he can smell Mommy, the furniture, the bed, the litter box, and my new collar, which Mommy put on me after I decided to become a housecat. It scratches my neck a little, and the bell still startles me sometimes when I move, but I know the collar means that I'm adopted, so I don't mind. Finishing his sniff, Fred backs off—still staring at me—then stretches, turns and saunters away. No touch of acceptance on my nose, but no hissing either.

I wait until I can no longer hear either of the boys' bells. Then I eat a little more, tiptoe into the TV room, and curl up beneath the sofa. Mommy and Ray walk through the kitchen, talking.

"That would have been, oh…six nights ago, I guess," Mommy says.

"And she's been inside ever since?" Ray asks, their voices growing closer.

"Except for the patio."

"And what about the litter box?"

"She uses it every time," Mommy answers happily. My whiskers rise with pride.

"Great!" Ray says. "And where is she now? Lucy girl!" he calls.

I scramble out from under the sofa, shaking my head to jangle my bell as they walk into the TV room. Ray comes over and picks me up. "I hear you're a full-fledged housecat now!" he says, stroking my head. "Daddy is very, very proud of you."

I lick the tip of his nose—a rough, affectionate lick. He chuckles and turns his face. I lick the side of his nose that is closest to me now. He turns the other way. I lick that side. He turns back and his eyes meet mine. I grab his cheeks with my paws to hold his face still so that I can provide him the kind of proper grooming that family cats give each other. "Lucy!" Daddy says. "You're going to take the skin right off my face!"

He puts me down, grinning.

For many moons after that, I work hard at becoming a
good family member, especially with the boys. I learn their
routine and follow it without protest. Beginning at breakfast,
I wait for the boys to eat, not taking my food until they are
finished, no matter how loudly my stomach growls. I spend as
much time as possible near them, but I never intrude on their
play. Instead, I watch quietly. I cover my waste thoroughly in
the litter box, just as my mother taught my siblings and me
to do when we squatted close together in a sheltered patch of
dirt. Ginger shovels the litter so often that you would think a
lone cat uses the box. But as my smells linger and mingle with
the aroma the boys leave behind, I begin to feel as though we
are littermates. I force myself to act like the runt, inviting them
to adopt me as their Mommy and Daddy have. I lie prone on
my stomach, my side, even my back, relaxed and docile when
we are in a room together, telling them that I am not a threat.
There is one rule they follow that I find very trying at
first—even though I know it is part of becoming a housecat.
We are allowed outside only on the patio, and only in the day-
time. There is no more strolling through the yards, wandering
down to the beach to watch Tevin work, studying the comings
and goings from the garage. "We want to keep you safe, Lucy
Miracle," Mommy explains. "So we can't just let you wander all
over the island."
Fred and Frisco lead the way onto the patio when we are
first let out in the morning. I follow at a respectful distance.
When we get there, Frisco turns and hisses at me. Then he and
Fred nose around together, catching the new morning's scents.
But Frisco doesn't stay outside long. As soon as he hears Tevin
or Ginger's cart pull up outside the hedge, he climbs back into
the house to his favorite place—on a soft towel tucked under

the bed. He comes out only when there aren't many humans around.

Fred wanders in and out all day, and I follow him. But even without Frisco around, Fred pretty much ignores me. There is plenty of room for us to have our own space on the patio. It's much larger than the deck and landing on which I used to live—as big as the living and eating rooms put together—and I am able to find amusements there. Trees sprout from circles of dirt cut into the stone. I practice my climbing, sinking my claws into the trees as far as they will go, hoisting myself further and further, and flopping backwards occasionally. But the trees are too tall for me to reach the top. I sharpen my claws on their bark and roll around in their shade. Leaves fall and dry in the sun. I pounce on them and kick them into the air, growling as though they are alive.

In a corner of the patio, there is a large cutout filled with sand. A stone turtle rises up from the sand, his head craning far out of his shell. I hop up on the turtle's back but my claws slip off, and I plummet down to the patio. His back is so slippery! His head is lower, so I give that a try and land safely on the turtle's snout, just beyond his bulging eyeballs. I creep carefully from his head to his tail and back again. I hang by my feet from his neck and then drop to the ground. I paw in the sand and scamper back and forth, imagining that I am on the beach.

The chairs on the patio are much softer than the chairs on the beach. Their cushions have brightly painted flowers on them. I lie on them to soak in the sun. When I want to feel the coolness of the stones on my stomach, I sprawl out underneath the chairs.

In one corner, a glistening post rises half a human high. Several strings hang from it. The strings are of different lengths, all of them above my head. Tied to the ends of the strings are lightweight fake birds—big birds, small birds, striped birds, solid birds, birds whose wings flap, birds whose beaks open and close when I bat them about. Mommy says, "Besides keeping *you* safe, Lucy, we want to protect the other island creatures. You don't need to hunt anymore—you get all the food you need. So you can stay here on the patio and *pretend* you're out chasing birds!"

How ridiculous, I think. Swatting at some flimsy fake bird is never going to replace the thrill of the hunt, the satisfaction of a big catch. But then I learn to appreciate the carefree luxury of walking into the house to eat my fill, then sauntering back out to the patio and slapping the toys around until I'm tired. I take a bath, licking my full belly, and remind myself that all the hunting my mother did was to calm our hunger. I remember when I escaped from the garage, how snagging that lizard was such an enormous accomplishment. I look at the briar hedge surrounding the patio that would rip my paw pads and cut my back if I were to try to escape, and somehow I don't mind the fake birds so much.

Late in the day, when the sun is disappearing behind the hedge, Mommy calls to us. "Dinner's ready!" We head to the laundry room, anticipating the fresh food in our bowls. We get moist food for breakfast and—if we don't eat it all at once—can nibble at it all day. For dinner, we get crunchy food. While we eat, Mommy closes the cat door, locking us in for the night.

But we don't get bored. There are toys in the house, too. Fake mice to swat around the floor, towers to climb, balls to bounce and chase, and posts to scratch our claws. Mommy sprinkles something that looks like dried seaweed on the base of one of the scratching posts. Catnip, it's called. "Fresh drugs," Mommy sings out, and the boys come running. They gobble up the flaky stuff and start rolling around, their feet in the air, purring wildly. I sniff at the catnip and cannot understand their excitement. It smells like pungent dried grass to me, not much different than the grass that grows on our island.

When the sky outside darkens, the lights in the house come on, and I hop up to the windowsill to see whether anyone is walking by. Although nighttime is when the island cats wander around freely, feeling safe in the stillness and cover of darkness, I am adjusting to the rhythms of a house-cat's life. When Mommy and Daddy are ready to sleep for the night, I find that I am, too. I follow them up the stairs, wanting to cuddle. But with the boys here, I don't even try to claim a permanent spot on the bed. Frisco clings like a suckling to Mommy's side and smacks me angrily, with his claws out, if I try to get near her. Daddy tries to protect me, putting me on the far side of his legs, away from Mommy and Frisco, but Frisco glares at me, making me too uneasy to sleep there, so I wander downstairs to a sofa or chair for the night.

The occasional lizard or palmetto bug runs by, and I chase it half-heartedly, without success. The sound of my bell precedes me, warning the prey. It becomes clear that my bell is for Mommy and Daddy, too. It helps them find me. Fred, Frisco, and I also keep track of each other by our jingling.

There's one advantage to being a housecat that I hadn't appreciated when I was living in my cage. I am privy to the most interesting conversations—much more talking than I was able to hear from my deck. And now that I wander the house freely, I can eavesdrop on any discussion that catches my ear. No one seems to mind.

I can be in the kitchen while Tevin and Ginger decide what food to serve. I can be in the office while Mommy or Daddy talk on the phone. I can be in the foyer when island workers come to discuss the pipe that's sprung a leak, or the golf cart that needs new wiring. I can be in the living room when visitors gather for drinks, passing on all sorts of island gossip.

"Did you hear that Timothy's house has been sold?" a visitor will ask.

Or, "I understand that Marjon is about to get fired," another will reveal.

I can lie under the dinner table while they continue their chitchat.

"Did you know that the mail boat is going to come by twice a week now?" someone asks.

Or, "I saw a bunch of cats at the feeders down by the power plant today," a visitor will tell Mommy. My ears always stand up at news of cats, hoping to catch every tidbit that I can.

When I hear a radio crackle, I can go into any room and listen to it. "RayDar, RayDar!" the radio calls out, Daddy and Mommy's names put together. Whoever is close by answers: "This is RayDar Tevin," or "This is RayDar Darcie." The voice in the radio is sometimes female and sometimes male, always human. It might report that the diving is especially good today because the water is clear or the nurse sharks are on the reef. It might announce that a package has arrived in the island office. It might invite Mommy and Daddy to someone else's house for dinner.

Most of the conversations I hear are happy ones, although humans squabble much more often than cats. Tevin and Ginger disagree over silly things like which plates to put on the table. Island workers debate which tool to use. Mommy and Daddy go on and on about their schedules, when to be where, and how to get things done.

"I have to get home by Wednesday for a board meeting,"

Mommy will say.

"I thought we could stay until Saturday!" Daddy complains.

"Really? I thought you had appointments on Thursday," Mommy answers.

"No, I changed them to Monday so that we could have a couple extra days here. I need to get more work done on the seawall," Daddy tells her.

"Well, I didn't know that," Mommy responds.

When I hear their voices getting louder, I rub up against their legs, meowing and batting my eyelashes. That usually calms them down.

I have yet to touch Ginger—or she me. On a cloudy afternoon, she rushes into the house, her voice as anxious as a mother hen's whose chick has just waddled onto a busy cart path. "Darr-say! Darr-say!" she calls.

Mommy must hear the urgency in her voice, too, because she flings open the door of the office so quickly that it sends a gust of air rushing by. "What is it?" she asks.

"I saw him!" Ginger says. "I talked to him!"

"Saw who?"

Ginger says the name that makes my whiskers bristle, and Mommy hurries into the living room.

"Where did you see him?"

"Down by the water tower. I was filling a feeder, and he drove up."

"Did he remember you from when you used to work for him?"

"Yes, he remember me," Ginger says, nodding her head, agitated. "He looked at me for a while, and I start getting nervous. I worked real slow, mopping out the feeder and filling the food and water, hoping he would go away—but he didn't."

"What did he do?"

"He drove closer and got off his cart. He walked right up to me. That man is whiter than I ever remember!" Ginger says. I picture the man with the hairy legs in the garage.

"Why *is* he so white?" Mommy asks.

"He doesn't like the sun," Ginger answers. "Even when he go fishing, he go in the early morning or the evening. When the sun shines, he hide in the house."

"Yeah, except for when he's chasing cats!" Mommy says. I hear a snarl in her voice.

"That's what he wanted to know about today: the cats."

"What about them?"

"All kind of things. He wants to know what I feed them and when. He wants to know how many cats we feed."

"What did you tell him?"

"I try not to tell him much. I tell him I feed them when I get time. I didn't say that I do it every morning. I tell him I don't know how many cats. And...he ask questions about me, too, why I take care of the cats."

"Well, it's part of your job! Did you tell him that?"

"Yes."

"And did you tell him you like to do it?"

"Yesss, but he laughs."

"Why would he laugh?"

"Well...there's something I never told you," Ginger confesses slowly.

"Oh. Are you going to tell me now?"

"Yes," Ginger says.

"So what is it?" Mommy asks, impatiently.

Ginger hangs her head, muffling her words. I head to a footstool closer to her, wanting to be sure of what I hear. I slip at the edge when I jump, catch myself and climb on. Mommy asks Ginger to repeat what she said. It sounds even more horrible this time.

"I help Uberan kill a cat when I work there."

"Helped him *kill* a cat? *You?* What did you do?"

"Well, you know I was afraid of cats," Ginger says, lifting her head. But she keeps her eyes on the ground. "So when he chase the cats away, I was glad. I didn't want them around either. Then one day he went after a cat with a shovel. It was just a little cat. It couldn't run fast enough. He whacked that cat right in the head."

"Oh my God," Mommy says. I cringe along with her. "Then what happened?"

"The cat was hurt bad," Ginger says. "It couldn't walk. It just lay on the steps wriggling. He told me to get rid of it and went back inside."

"What did you do?"

"I checked on it every few minutes, and it just lay there, wriggling and wriggling."

"Was it crying?"

"No, it didn't make any noise. Kind of like it was wriggling in its sleep, only I figured it was dying, so I go and got Evanko," Ginger says. "He worked next door. I brought him back with me and showed him the cat. He put a rag over its head, and then Evanko hit it in the head with the shovel again. It stopped moving."

"Oh Ginger," Mommy says, but she's not mad. A tear is seeping into her eyelashes. "Then what?"

"He heard the sound of the shovel, and he come outside. He pick up the rag and look at the cat. Its head was all bloody and bashed in." Ginger's voice trails off. "Then, he told me I did a good job and went back inside. Evanko take the cat and bury it." Ginger finally lifts her eyes to meet Mommy's. "I felt terrible. The next day, I start looking for another house to work in. There was no reason to be afraid of that little cat. I still don't touch cats, but I never ever hurt another one, never ever. And

I would not."

Mommy breathes in, so hard it makes a whistling noise, and stands perfectly still, staring at Ginger. Ginger drops her head back down. The ticking of the clock seems to ricochet off the living room walls. Then Ginger lifts her eyes to Mommy's face and breaks the silence. Her sentences come out in a rush, tumbling onto each other like kittens chasing a leaf.

"I tell him that I like to feed the cats. I tell him I like to see them happy. I tell him I'm sorry about that cat at his house and that I never hurt another cat. I tell him that cats don't hurt anyone. I tell him about Fred and Frisco and Lucy. I tell him to *stop trapping cats!*"

"Oh my gosh, Ginger!" Mommy interrupts. "Did he ask you how you know he's trapping cats?"

"Nooo...he stops laughing and just listened. He stared at me, strange. He doesn't ask any questions. Then he just drove away. I come back here fast, to tell you."

"Why did you think it was so important to tell me right away?" Mommy asks.

"Because I'm worried about him," Ginger says. "There's no telling what he will do. What if he puts poison in the cat food?"

"You mean the cat food in the *feeders?*"

"Yes."

"Oh, I don't want to believe that anyone would be sick enough to do that! The feeders are helping him! Freeman says there are fewer cats on his property, and I'm sure it's because the cats aren't hungry." Mommy pauses. "Have you seen any sign that the cats aren't feeling well? Are they still coming around, the same as ever?"

"Yes," Ginger answers. "Everything is fine...but he's seen a feeder now."

"Oh, he's seen the feeders for a long time, Ginger. He only stopped to talk to you. He probably couldn't believe his eyes—that someone so afraid of cats was out there feeding them. Don't you think so?" Mommy asks.

"Maybe..." Ginger says.

"Well, from now on, why don't you go around to the feeders a couple more times each day," Mommy tells her. "Not to fill them each time...just drive by them and take a look. See whether the cats are still jumping in and out of them the same as always; see whether they still look healthy. If you see *any* sign *whatsoever* that any of the cats aren't feeling well, you tell me *immediately!* Okay?"

"Yes," Ginger answers.

"And I'll pay more attention too," Mommy says. "I like to stop and watch the cats, just because I enjoy it. So I ought to notice if anything unusual is going on."

"Okay," Ginger says. "And Darr-say ..." her voice trails off.

"Yes?" Mommy prompts her.

"I am very sorry about that cat. I would never hurt a cat."

"Oh, Ginger, I know you wouldn't," Mommy says, putting an arm around her shoulders. "It's okay. You did the best you knew at the time. You knew that kitten was dying and you wanted Evanko to put her out of her misery. If you were to see a hurt kitty today, I know that you would get help right away. And I'm sorry that you ever had to work for such a horrible man."

I think about the way Ginger treats the boys and me. She doesn't pet us, but she talks to us, always greeting us with a "Good morning," and leaving us with a "Good night." If she sees that our bowls are empty, she sneaks us a little extra food. She washes our biggest bowl often, filling it with clear, cool water. And she doesn't seem to mind cleaning our litter box, not a bit. I often regret that I caused her so much trouble when I lived on the sofa. Sometimes I even think about rubbing against Ginger's legs, just to let her know that I'm sorry, but

I've always been pretty sure she wouldn't like it. Now, I hop down and walk over to Ginger, stopping just short of her feet, looking up at her, Mommy's arm still around her shoulders. "Mrreow," I say, lowering my eyelids until they are almost shut, then opening them as slowly as I can.

Ginger looks down at me. "Thank you, Lucy Miracle," she says.

"Mrreow," I answer.

At night, when the dinner guests are gone and the house is quiet, Mommy tells Daddy about her talk with Ginger. Her voice is hushed and serious. Daddy's voice is tight. He says things like "could really be dangerous" and "like to put *him* in a trap." Mommy presses her finger against his lips. I wish that I could go and cuddle between them, make my fuzzy wuzzy eyes at Daddy. But Frisco is burrowed next to Mommy, as usual. I stay on a rug in the farthest corner of the room, watching, until I fall asleep.

Every sunrise, my whiskers lift with the hope that this may be the day the boys and I become friends. But Fred remains standoffish, and—when the house is silent enough for him to be out and about—Frisco can be downright hostile. He steals up on me from behind, hissing and nipping, the way a lizard sneaks up on a fly and grabs it by the tail end of its wings. At least he can't eat me the way a lizard eats his prey, slow crunch by slow crunch, the lizard's throat opening and closing, gulp by gulp, while the fly's bulging red eyeballs stare out of the lizard's mouth, helplessly watching the world fade away.

I try many ingenious hiding places: behind the trash can, under the desk, squeezed between office machines, beneath the sofa, up on a ledge. But Frisco searches me out wherever I am, reaching behind furniture, around obstacles and between objects to swat at me, determined to let me know that this house is his and that I am not welcome here. I eventually learn that the safest tactic is to perch on the highest point I can muster, maybe a stool in the kitchen, or on a step halfway up the staircase overlooking the living room. If I am not at eye level, Frisco seems to feel that I am not actually invading his turf, plus he has to work harder to get to me.

From these high vantage points, I can also watch Fred and Frisco. They are the best of friends—litter brothers, raised together just like my siblings and I were—and yet you wouldn't necessarily know it from watching. Sometimes they walk by each other companionably, maybe stopping to touch noses or take a quick sniff; sometimes they chat and sniff each other. Frisco's "meow" is higher pitched than Fred's and often has a note of complaint to it. "Mrrreeeeow?" he demands, nosing Fred's backside and paws to try and smell where he's been. Fred is patient with Frisco, even indulgent. He answers with a quick "mrrrow," and allows Frisco a thorough sniff. Sometimes the boy cats ignore each other; sometimes, they lie on the floor side-by-side, stretched out and peaceful. And lots of times, they tussle.

If Fred is walking or sitting on the floor, Frisco climbs on top of him from behind, like a crab climbing up to sit on a rock. Frisco uses his front legs like a crab's pincers, planting them just outside of Fred's back legs, trying to keep him still. He growls and sinks his teeth into the nape of Fred's neck, right at the tough spot where a mother picks up her kittens. Then he positions his back legs on either side of Fred's tail and starts pawing at the floor with them. Fred sits passively through this whole process, staring straight ahead, letting Frisco dominate him, until he's had enough. Then he shakes Frisco loose, turns around and swats him, and a wrestling match begins.

The boys roll on the floor, jabbing their teeth and claws into each other, but not deeply enough to hurt. They thrash around like fishes until one or the other gets tired. Sometimes the tired cat will simply stop moving, like a fish that has been pulled out of water and taken its last gasp on the dock. More often, the brother who's tired will start licking the other, calming him down and signaling peace.

It's not just Frisco who starts the brawls. Occasionally Fred attacks first, climbing up on Frisco in exactly the same way. When Fred is on top, Frisco goes limp on the floor, all splayed out. Then Fred uses his teeth to haul Frisco by the neck across the slick floor tiles, as though he's dragging the carcass of a bird underneath a bush.

I sit on my perch and study these interactions, a strange but compelling mix of love and fighting. Island cats have no time for such romps. The most my mother ever managed was a playful swat, or maybe an affectionate nip at our bellies after we nursed. She needed every iota of her strength to hoist herself back up and resume the hunt for our next meal.

A genuine conflict is rare as well. Island cats need to co-operate to find food and to dodge human treachery. The only clash I ever witnessed was between two tomcats screeching and spitting in the night over a mate.

The first time I witness the boys faking a fight, my own resentment surprises me—resentment that they can afford to squander their energy this way, when my mother and the other island cats have to work so hard. But then I remember the feeders, and my bitterness vanishes as quickly as the boys' phony anger. My mother's tummy is probably as full as mine is now. Maybe she has leisure time to roll around in the grass, playing as the boys do. When their fights are over, they act as though nothing has happened, Fred making his way out the door, Frisco strolling to his bowl for another meal, sometimes reaching up and taking a swat in my direction, just for good measure.

One morning, when the humans are on the beach and the house is quiet with napping cats, I make my move. I've been planning, watching Fred and Frisco, working on my strategy. Now—while Fred is stretched out on the floor of the big living room, his eyes closed, his tail gently swishing with dreams—is the time.

I stand up quietly on the sofa and—pounce! I jump to the floor next to Fred. I drape one of my front legs over the back of his neck, pinning him down. Then I start licking his head: his ears, forehead, eyes, whiskers. Just when he's completely relaxed and enjoying the bath, his eyes shut and his head bobbing, I take my first jab. It's a sharp one, my free paw to his chest, claws in, while I clamp down with my other leg and bite the side of his neck.

My strategy works perfectly.

Fred, startled, snaps his eyes open and jerks his head up. He throws his ears back, and from the way he narrows his eyes, I can see that he is thinking about walloping me—but he doesn't. Instead, he relaxes his ears, rolls over on his back and thrusts at me with both of his front paws, vigorously but playfully, claws in. I lower just the tips of my front teeth into his chest, and stretch myself out on top of his stomach. My whole length reaches only to his middle.

Fred bites me on the ear, just hard enough to get my attention. I roll off him and sit up, towering over him while he lies, belly up, on the floor. I paste my ears against my skull and stare at him, unblinking. He locks onto my gaze as I dance around his head, sidestepping, tail twitching. Fred's tail thumps against the floor, a dull slow beat as I circle him.

Fred makes the next move, a quick punch to my ear. Again I fall on him, flopping down hard, and now we entwine our entire bodies and roll over and over, punching with our paws and nipping with our teeth. After a few rolls, I jump off, straighten my ears, and give Fred a few friendly licks on the top of his head; then I jump up on the sofa, nonchalantly, and start giving myself a bath.

Fred stands up, stretches, and ambles off into the kitchen without looking at me, as though nothing has happened between us. As I lift a hind leg and twist my head to scrub it, I see Frisco, crouched in the dining room doorway, watching.

My plan is completely fulfilled. Frisco has witnessed our good-natured scrap and has seen that I am now his equal in at least one way: I am an official playmate of Fred's.

Mommy is dumping crunchy dinner food into our bowls when the radio sputters to life in the kitchen. Ginger is washing dishes; Tevin has gone to his cottage for a shower.

"RayDar, RayDar Darcie." Daddy sounds urgent. "RayDar, RayDar Darcie!"

Mommy sets the food bag down and hurries to the radio. "RayDar Darcie," she answers.

"Go to stealth," he tells her.

"Going to stealth," Mommy says. The radio emits a series of electronic beeps as she switches the channel. "RayDar Ray," she says into the speaker. "Go ahead."

"I'm in a meeting at the airport and I just saw Freeman drive by, heading your way," Daddy says. "He has a cat on the back of his cart."

"Okay," Mommy answers. "We're here! Thank you."

"Not okay!" Daddy comes back. "Uberan is following him."

"Oh, no!" Mommy's voice is suddenly concerned. "Does Freeman know?"

"I doubt it. He seemed oblivious, and Uberan is keeping his distance."

"Thanks for the warning," Mommy says. "Are you coming home?"

"Just as soon as I can break away," Daddy says. "Call if you need me. Let's stay on this channel."

"Okay," says Mommy. "Staying on stealth."

The boys are eating, but when I hear a golf cart pull into the garage, I am too curious to wait for my turn at dinner. I follow Mommy to the groaning door and hide just inside the little office next to it. As she opens the door, I hear a second golf cart pull in, brakes screeching. "FREEMAN!" a man shouts. Mommy steps into the garage. Voices mingle: the loud man, Freeman, Mommy. But I can't make out the words. Ginger creeps to my side of the door, drying her hands on a dishtowel. She cracks it open so that we both can hear.

"...at my urging," Mommy is saying. "Freeman is very loyal to you, and I had to beg him. I had to convince him that what we're doing is much better for cat control than killing them!"

"I *knew* he wasn't killing them," the man says, not as loudly. "I've seen him drive away with a live cat on his cart before. Mosey says he brought a dead one to the incinerator, but I don't believe it."

Freeman starts to say something, but Mommy cuts him off. "Would you like to come in and talk about it, Mr. Uberan?" she asks. Ginger eases the door shut and hurries back to the kitchen, her ankles barely missing my ears.

I scurry into the TV room and under the sofa. I hear the garage door open wide, and footsteps walk toward me. Frisco's bell rings riotously as he bolts for the far end of the house. "Have a seat," Mommy says, and right in front of me, dark boots settle on the floor as the weight of a human sitting down makes the sofa sag above me. The bare, pale legs are within clawing distance. They are even hairier up close. The fur down the middle of my back fluffs and rises, a bushy stripe from head to tail. There is no doubt now: Uberan *is* the man I freed from the garage! Instinct urges me to lash out and rip his papery thin skin. I imagine the blood dribbling down, faster than the drops that fell from his broken finger—how bright and satisfying it would look against that flesh, instantly curdling around the hairs as the legs jump up and run away. But I battle my impulse, forcing myself to remain motionless.

Mommy sits on the other end of the sofa. I see Freeman's lightweight pants as he settles into a chair across the room.

"I know that you've been on the island a long time, Mr. Uberan," Mommy says, "and that the cats have probably pestered you quite a lot in the past."

"Pester is not the word for it!" he retorts. "Torment is more like it. They're like little rats running around. Those cats used to crawl all over my yard and howl all night long."

"Used to!" Mommy echoes. "That's right! That was because they were starving and desperate to find food. And they howled in the night because they were looking for mates. All of that is changing." She tells Uberan about spaying and neutering the island cats. "Now, they don't have the urge to reproduce. They can just hang out together and be friends." She explains how the feeders work. Fred settles in across the room to listen. I can see his full body, stretched out on the floor. "...so that's why you're getting so few cats on your property these days. Freeman has only captured five, six including the one on his cart right now. The cats simply don't need to search for food or to hunt the way they used to. Most of them go to their feeders in the morning, play and snooze during the day, and go back to eat some more in the evening."

"That doesn't stop them from being disgusting, dirty creatures," Uberan shudders.

"Oh, Mr. Uberan." Mommy smiles. "Cats are extremely

clean creatures. They hate to be dirty. Their tongues are like washcloths—specifically made for bathing—and that's what they do for much of the day, especially when they have plenty to eat and don't have to be out prowling for a meal! They're even tidy with their bathroom habits: they find a nice sandy spot out of the way, dig a deep hole, and cover it up when they're done."

As if on cue, Fred lifts a paw and dampens it with his tongue, then begins to wash his mouth. He moves on to his whiskers, his nose, his eyes, noisily lapping at his paw and wiping it all over his face. He wets his knuckle and digs it into his ears, moving from one to the other. He scrubs his ears so hard I can hear them crackle. Then he twists his head to reach his shoulders. He cuts through his fur with his teeth, letting them settle all the way onto his skin. He gurgles as he releases some saliva, and combs his teeth back upward through the fur. In between strokes, he thumps his tail loudly on the floor. He pretends not to notice Uberan—or anyone else—acting completely engrossed in his bath.

After a few thumps, Uberan insults us again. "But they carry diseases!" he says.

"Lots of people used to think that. But it's not true," Mommy assures him. "We've taken blood samples from all the cats we've spayed and neutered, and there are no illnesses. No rabies, no leukemia, no FIV—no diseases, period. These are healthy cats. Lots of them used to look sickly because they were so emaciated from hunting and not finding enough food. And their fur would be all matted because they barely had the stamina to bathe. All their energy went into just trying to stay alive."

"So how long will it take until they all die?" Uberan asks.

"Die? What do you mean?" Mommy asks.

"Until they all die off because they can't make any more

kittens."

"Oh!" Mommy hesitates. I suck in my breath, and then I remember Mommy saying there would always be some kittens on our island. But please don't tell Uberan that! I think. He wants them all gone!

"Well," Mommy replies, "that could take years. But remember, during those years you'll see the cats less and less. They'll get into the habit of staying in their own territories, once they know they can find everything they need there. Before long, you'll practically have to go searching for a cat to find one, except around the feeders."

Ginger walks into the room, right in the middle of Mommy's conversation with Uberan. I have never seen her interrupt before. "Hello, Mr. Uberan," she greets him. "May I get you something to drink?"

"No thank you, Ginger," he answers. "I'm fine."

Oh no, you are not, I think. I scrunch my claws into their sockets.

"How about you, Freeman?" she asks.

"I'm all right," he says.

"Thank you," Mommy says, her tone dismissing Ginger.

But Ginger doesn't leave. Instead, she walks over to Fred. From my vantage point under the sofa, I see her feet stop beside him and her hand reach down to pat him on the head—just a couple of awkward taps on the hard top of his skull, right between the ears. It makes a gentle slapping noise. Fred looks up at her, startled. Uberan clears his throat.

The garage door opens.

"Hi there!" Daddy calls jovially. "How you doin', Freeman?" I hear them shake hands.

Uberan stands up as Daddy turns toward him. "You must be Mr. Uberan," he says. "I've seen you a time or two on the road, but haven't had the opportunity to make your acquaintance. It's nice to meet you."

"Uh-huh," Uberan mumbles.

"I'd shake your hand," Daddy says, "but by the looks of that bandage, your hand wouldn't appreciate it."

"Right," Uberan says, declining to explain the bandage. I picture his bloodied finger after I released it, crooked and dangling.

Daddy sits down on a chair beside Mommy. Uberan settles into the sofa above me again. This time, his hat hangs from his hands, between his knees. He fiddles with the hat, holding it first by the brim, then turning it over and fingering it along the edge with his good hand. The bandage looks like a thick caterpillar, thrusting awkwardly off into the air.

"To what do we owe the pleasure of this visit?" Daddy asks.

"Mr. Uberan and I were just talking about the island cats," Mommy answers.

"Oh! Great looking cats, aren't they?" Daddy enthuses. "Have you seen how healthy they are these days, Mr. Uberan? They're all getting fat, I'm afraid. Too much to eat...before long, we'll have to put them on a diet!" Daddy chuckles.

Uberan coughs. His hat starts turning over faster. "Well, actually," Uberan begins, and coughs again, "I have no use for cats. Don't like them at all, in fact."

"Oh, too bad!" Daddy jumps in. "That's probably because you don't know any cats up close and personal. Why, Ginger didn't like cats either, when we met her! Isn't that right, Ginger?"

"Yesss," Ginger answers. Her laced-up shoes are still beside Fred. I can see her legs, up to her knees.

"But now," Mommy takes over, "Ginger has gotten to know cats. She's learned how harmless they are. She feeds the island cats, and she loves our cats. Isn't that right, Ginger?"

"Yesss," Ginger answers, as her hand cuffs Fred's skull

again. He stands up and stretches, raising his back to meet her fingers.

"And the cats love her, too!" Daddy adds.

"Hmmph!" Uberan says. "A cat can't love anybody. But I did see Ginger at a feeder the other day. I wouldn't have believed that she would get that close to cats, if I hadn't seen it with my own eyes. And take Freeman here! Best worker I ever had, reliable as the day is long—flat out disobeying me. And you folks. I can't understand what you're thinking. You've got enough stuff in your garage to feed a *couple* of islands full of cats."

"Speaking of the garage..." Daddy interrupts, and Mommy coughs loudly, cutting him off.

I hurry to the other end of the couch, beneath Mommy. I strut out into the open and eyeball Uberan. A look of recognition crosses his face, as quickly as a hummingbird flitting by, before he erases it and glances away from me. I stroll over to Ginger. She doesn't move a muscle as I rub my fur against her legs. I start with my shoulders and brush the length of my body against her, all the way to my tail. I do it again, a more leisurely rub this time. I feel Ginger's calf twitch. Then Fred and I sit down together. I start bathing his face. Fred purrs loudly.

All the humans are watching us, including Uberan. I recognize the confusion in his eyes. I continue bathing Fred as Uberan speaks again.

"So, if all of you are so determined to save the cats on Cat Cay, I won't fight you—for now. But I want those cats to stay *off* my property! If they don't, my cooperation ends," he warns.

"Well, Mr. Uberan, we can't promise that there will never be another cat wandering across your yard," Mommy tells him. "But we're doing our best—if you could please just be patient with us."

"I've been patient with those cats for far too long, but Freeman can put the traps away for the time being," Uberan answers, staring at Fred and me. Then he looks at Freeman. "They were a waste of time anyway!"

"No, they weren't. Freeman accomplished most of what you wanted," Mommy defends him. "Word about your traps has probably gotten around among the cats—they have a way of learning these things, you know. It'll help keep them away."

"Okay," Uberan says, standing up. "I'll give you a little while, and see what happens."

Freeman is standing now as well. "Thank you, sir," he says.

"Thank you, Mr. Uberan," Daddy says. "If you have any more concerns about the cats, just give us a shout. And you're always welcome at our house. Anything you want to see or talk about, just ask. No need…" Mommy nudges him with her elbow. Uberan fiddles with his bandage. Daddy doesn't finish his sentence.

Mommy begins to lead Uberan to the garage, putting a hand on his shoulder. He stiffens. She drops her hand and opens the door. Her good-bye gets lost in its creaking. "Bye," Uberan answers, curtly.

Mommy closes the door and leans her back against it, hands behind her, still clasping the doorknob. "Good job, Ginger!" she calls out softly, smiling. "You okay after touching Fred?" she teases. Ginger chortles. "And you too, Freeman," Mommy adds. "Thank you both so much!"

"And *you*," she says to Daddy, "quite the charmer! Until you almost blew it."

"Oh, I wasn't really going to mention his sneaky visit to the garage," Daddy says. "Maybe just let him know that I'm aware of it." He smiles and gives Mommy a little hug.

I walk over to Mommy, anticipating that she will congratulate my cleverness in rubbing against Ginger. "Mreeow,"

I say, coaxing her. She leans over and picks me up. She kisses my head, but doesn't offer a single word of praise for me—or Fred!—even though I ask her to again: "Mrrreeow!" Instead, she talks with Freeman as she walks him to the garage. I am in the crook of her arm when the door opens. On the back of Freeman's cart is a trap with a towel on top.

As Freeman walks around the cart to climb into the driver's seat, he tugs at the towel to tighten it. The edge of the towel closest to me jerks up, and I see the cat crouching in the trap. She has grown plump, but the dark outline of her eyes is unmistakable. There's the familiar sandy patch on her cheek, shaped like a sand dollar. The crooked ear, dark at the bottom and pale at the tip. Her beautiful, straight ear looks different—it has a notch at the top, like mine. Her dusty smell is still the same. My mother!

I jump from Mommy's arm to the floor of the garage, racing toward the trap. My mother raises her head and crawls toward me. I sink back on my hind legs, preparing to launch myself onto the cart. I leap forward and catch the floorboard with my claws, just as the cart pulls away. The sudden motion flings me off, and throws my mother backwards against the metal bars of the cage. She howls. Freeman reaches back and rests his arm on top of the trap, steadying it. The cart picks up speed. The edge of the towel flaps in the wind.

I gallop down the driveway, chasing the cart. Behind me, Mommy hollers, "Lucy! Lucy Miracle!" I keep running. The distance between the cart and me widens. I force my legs to stretch further, race faster. I focus on my mother. When Freeman reaches the end of the driveway, he slows, and I begin to close the gap. Closer, closer…then Freeman guns the cart. Its motor whines as the cart turns onto the road. Mommy is running right behind me. "Lucy! Come back here, Lucy!"

I sprint out of the driveway and down the street, but by the time I reach the edge of our yard, the cart has already pulled a house and lawn ahead of me. I try to run faster, but my legs are already working as hard as they can and I am almost out of breath. From a road that branches off to the side, I see a cart closing in on me—Uberan's! He turns the corner so quickly that I can feel his draft on the whiskers of my legs. I lunge beneath a plumbago bush as Uberan yells from the speeding cart, "FREEMAN! FREEMAN! STOP!"

Freeman's head jerks around as he slams on the brakes. Uberan hits his brakes, too, and yanks the wheel. Tires screech as he plows into the corner of Freeman's cart. A headlight shatters and glass sprays onto the road. The cage with my mother in it bounces off the seat and topples after the glass. She screams as she hits the ground, and then goes silent. She lies twisted and still against the bars of the upended cage.

Mommy rushes past me and Uberan, who is still sitting in his cart. She kneels beside my mother and turns the cage right side up. My mother's body slides downward with the motion, until she is lying in the bottom of the cage, her head lolling against the side rails. Freeman gets off his cart and walks toward Mommy.

"Freeman, *where* are you going with that cat?" Uberan demands of him, not looking at my mother, ignoring the fact that she is now lying motionless in the road.

"Is she okay?" asks Freeman.

"I don't know," answers Mommy. She pokes her fingers through the bars of the cage and prods my mother, gently. I creep closer, still under cover of the plumbago branches.

"*Freeman!*" Uberan snaps. "*Where* are you going with that cat?"

"I was taking her back to release her," Freeman answers him.

"Not to *my* yard, you're not!" Uberan says.

"No, sir," Freeman assures him. "I was going to let her go in her territory, near the feeder."

"Fine, then—but remember: I do not want to see another cat in my yard!"

"Yes, sir," Freeman answers, wearily.

Uberan straightens his tires, then backs up and wheels around Freeman's cart, swerving to avoid the shattered glass. He disappears down the road.

Mommy's hand is still inside the cage, scratching my mother's ears. I walk to the cage and thrust my face between the bars, trying to reach my mother's nose. I feel her breath on my whiskers. I stretch out my tongue as far as it will go, and manage to graze just the tip of her nose. She opens her eyes, groggily, and struggles to focus on my face. Mommy puts her other hand inside the cage and runs it up and down the length of my mother's body, along her sides and her back. When she reaches under her stomach, my mother's eyes convey alarm. I lick the tip of her nose again, to let her know that it is okay for the human to touch her. My mother shuts her eyes, wearily, and submits to Mommy's handling.

"She's conscious," Mommy says. "And there's no blood or other sign of injury that I can see. Apparently nothing is broken, but she's certainly shaken up. I wish we had a vet on the island, so I could get her checked out."

"I'll take her home," says Freeman.

"Oh, no, I don't think you should release her until we know she's okay," Mommy tells him.

"I know, I know," Freeman says. "I didn't mean to her home—I mean take her home with me."

"Where? To your cottage?"

"Yes," Freeman says. "I can watch her for a while, make sure she's okay, up and moving around, and then set her free."

"That's a great idea," Mommy says. "And if she doesn't

come around, or if you need any help, call me on the radio. In fact, I'd like to look at her before you let her go, if you don't mind."

"All right, okay, I'll call you," Freeman tells her.

My mother's eyes are open but still unfocused as Freeman lifts her cage and puts it in the cart—this time, on the front seat with him.

Mommy picks me up as they drive away, and begins to scold me. "Lucy girl! You must *never* run into the road! What would we do if you got hurt?" She hugs me tightly and rubs her scent against my whiskers.

I compel myself to stop gazing down the now empty street. I lick Mommy's nose. But I don't speak. There is no cat language to make her understand. I settle into her arms as she carries me back into the house.

That night, I work extra hard at my communication skills with humans. I like to practice when we have visitors.

"How did you find Cat Cay?" one of tonight's guests asks Mommy and Daddy. I've seen them before—a man named Frederique and a woman named Dahlia, both with hair the color of whitecaps in the ocean on a windy day. They have their own house on the island. I am curled up on the windowsill, listening.

"We came here when we first started boating," Mommy answers. "It was a convenient place to clear customs into the Bahamas because it's so close to Florida. We planned to overnight here, then be on our way."

"But Darcie couldn't stay on the boat—or even in the marina. She had to trespass!" Daddy says.

Mommy rolls her eyes at him. "I did *not* intend to trespass," she insists. "I didn't see the sign, so I didn't know that this was a private island. I just got off the boat and went for a walk, like I do wherever we dock. It was late afternoon and sunny, but once I got past the marina, I didn't see another soul. The island was so quiet it seemed deserted. And yet it was so manicured—I was absolutely dazzled by the landscaping! All the beautiful lawns, the hedges bursting with hibiscus flowers, the bougainvillea climbing the trees...

"By the time I came to the pool, I was completely in love. There it was, overlooking that white sand beach and turquoise sea, the pool water sparkling, clearer and bluer than the ocean, with the overhead fans whirring above the tables—as though the Great Gatsby had just wrapped up a party and everyone had gone home."

"Yeah sure, she didn't see the sign! Reporters. They think they own the world!" Daddy teases, and everyone laughs.

I learn a lot about Mommy and Daddy from conversations like these. Mommy used to work "in television...doing the news," she says. Daddy did something called technology, making computers and other machines that humans use. That got them more money than they needed for food, so they could buy a big boat and explore places I'd never heard about, and find my island and get a house here, and teach me to be a housecat.

"How much time do you spend here?" I hear Mommy ask.

"About a third of the year," Dahlia answers, "although it's unusual for us to be here this late in the season. We actually need to get back home soon!"

"Home." The word pricks at me like a thorn on a bougainvillea bush, a signal to jump off the windowsill and into Mommy's lap.

Now that I am a housecat, it is especially depressing when my humans and Fred and Frisco go "home," back to the place they call Florida, leaving me behind. The days have lengthened again, so I visit the patio only in the mornings, before the sun is high and scorching. The house is cool, but achingly empty with only Tevin and Ginger as occasional company. So I work hard to keep my family here, trying to make them love me so much that they'll never want to leave.

For instance, I talk a lot. Humans seem to like that. I meow when I want someone to follow me (a long drawn out mrrreeowww); when I want to be fed (a few sharp, repetitive meows with a bit of a "please" in them); when I want to be picked up (head cocked upward and my meow loud and aimed at the human in question); when I want to say hello, or to let someone know that I'm near them (a long lazy meeeoww as I stretch, lengthening my front legs and sinking my head down onto my knees); or when I want to be let through a door (a little chirping meow that is combined with my rolling over on my back and waving my paws in the door's general direction).

"Look at her being cute," Mommy or Daddy will say when I do my rolling over.

"Being cute is not going to make that door open," they'll admonish. But I know better because more often than not, it does. Being cute works for lots of things, especially for getting attention and petting. So does bathing the humans. Mommy and Daddy love to have their faces washed, especially Mommy. Why don't I try that now?

I climb up on her chest, put my front paws on her shoulders, and start washing her nose.

"Oh, my!" Dahlia says. "Do you like that?" she asks, her wrinkled nose suggesting that she would not.

"Yes," Mommy answers, smiling. "It's a sign of affection, and I look at it as free dermabrasion—Lucy has the roughest cat tongue I've ever felt!"

"Well, in that case, it might save some money at the

doctor's office!" Dahlia says. "What happened to her ear?" she asks.

"When we spay and neuter the island cats, the vet puts a notch in their ears," Daddy tells her. "That way, if a cat with a notched ear gets trapped again, we'll know to let it go."

"I'm thinking about putting a little diamond stud in Lucy's notch—what do you think, Ray?" Mommy says this just to annoy him—I can tell, because she's said it before, and always with a little laugh in her voice. Daddy rolls his eyes each time, and they never put anything in my ear.

"It would be beautiful on her!" Dahlia says. "She has such gorgeous eyes—it looks like she's wearing eyeliner. And she's so small and dainty!"

I jump down from Mommy's lap and walk over to Dahlia, favoring her with a leisurely brush on the legs, a maneuver that most humans seem especially susceptible to. I weave in and out between her feet, rubbing both of her legs and wrapping my tail around them, just a little bit, for a gentle tickle. Sure enough, she reaches down to pet me, scratching my back, touching my tail as it twirls around her ankle. I purr, loudly enough for her to hear.

"She is an affectionate thing, isn't she?" Dahlia asks.

Encouraged, I decide to visit Dahlia's lap. But just as I hop up to join her on the chair, Dahlia crosses her legs. Instead of landing on the chair cushion, I catch her knee as it swings by my chest. Reflexively, my claws thrust out to try and stop my tumbling body. They catch in her pant leg and I pull a small piece of fabric with me as I fall back to the floor.

"Oh, my!" Dahlia exclaims. She rubs her knee as I scamper to Daddy and crouch down beside him.

"I am so sorry!" Mommy says, rushing to Dahlia. She eyes her pants, the thread dangling from knee to floor. "I'm afraid Lucy snagged your slacks while she was trying to jump in your lap. Are you hurt?"

"Not at all," says Dahlia. "I didn't see her jumping up, just moved at the wrong time."

"Lucy often thinks she can jump a little higher than is realistic for her size," Mommy says. I sink my chin onto my paws, annoyed but not daring to leave the room, afraid to make another misstep. "I am terribly sorry about your slacks," Mommy adds.

"Oh, these old things," Dahlia says. "I've had them for years, got them in the boutique way back when."

Frederique changes the subject. "How many cats do you think we have on the island?" he asks.

"That's impossible to say," Mommy answers, sitting down, "because we never see them all at once. But from the numbers we captured for TNR, I would guess that there are easily over a hundred."

A hundred. I turn the phrase over in my head. I can't picture a hundred. Has my mother—a member of that hundred—recovered yet? Will she be set free once again? And does she wander alone, with a notch in her ear and no more kittens to keep her company? Or does she have a companion? Oh, if only she and the other island cats knew how easy it is to train humans!

"We're going through about sixty pounds of cat food a week," Daddy says, "if that gives you any indication."

At night, when I watch out the window for other island cats, I can see that the easy-to-find food has had an effect. The cats' steps are slower. Their tails are relaxed. They are not on the hunt; they are out rambling. I see them walk by seagulls, mourning doves, even sparrows searching the ground for bugs, with barely a glance. And their bodies are bigger, their bellies hang lower, their fur is shinier.

"We don't see as many cats as we used to," Dahlia says.

"They used to be crawling all over the island, scrawny things."

"Well, we don't want to wipe out the entire island population," Mommy says. "But with fewer litters, there will certainly be fewer cats. And now that they're not begging in people's yards, or climbing over the trash cans, most people seem to have made peace with them—some are donating money to help us feed them!"

"Even Uberan says he'll try to put up with the cats," Daddy adds.

My whiskers prickle just the slightest bit as Frederique says, "Don't trust Uberan! He doesn't even like *people*, let alone cats. Remember that time Uberan got mad at Lionel because he nicked his boat while he was docking?" he asks, looking at Dahlia.

Dahlia nods.

"Next morning, Lionel's boat was floating up the channel. Somebody had untied it in the middle of the night. They never could pin it on Uberan."

Dahlia shakes her head. "He is not a nice man. It's a wonder he's lasted on Cat Cay."

"It's only because he keeps to himself," Frederique says.

Tevin pokes his head through the door from the kitchen. "Dinner is served," he announces.

The humans stand up, headed for the dining room. I follow them. But Mommy stops me. "You *stay*, please, Lucy, and we'll see you after dinner," Mommy says, bending and touching me on the nose with one long finger.

At her touch, I plop my hind end right down on the floor, immediately, the way I learned from watching Fred. "Good girl, Lucy!" Mommy says. At least I did that right, I think, and stay put as the humans walk away. Then I jump into Mommy's warm spot on the sofa and fall asleep, dreaming of mounds and mounds of cat food, piled up on tree stumps, cisterns, golf cart paths and everywhere. The island cats encircle the mounds, purring and munching away.

I am still on the sofa, stretching and pondering whether to get up for a snack, when Frederique and Dahlia leave, crossing paths on the doorstep with Freeman. When he walks into the house, I am instantly awake and sitting up. Freeman is carrying the trap. Its bottom is covered with a soft towel. My mother is stretched out on the towel, her eyes closed.

"She crawled around for a little while," Freeman tells Mommy and Daddy, "but she didn't meow or cry, and she didn't seem to be in any pain. I thought she'd gone to sleep, so I slipped in this towel to make her feel more comfortable—but that was hours ago, and she's never come to. She doesn't move, not even if I touch her. I thought you'd better take a look."

"Good idea, Freeman," Mommy tells him. "It's possible that she has internal injuries that we can't see. Why don't you let us keep her, and I'll take her to the island doctor as soon as the clinic opens in the morning, before we leave for Florida. If there's something obviously wrong, maybe he can help her. If not, we'll have to think about trying to get her into the states with us, for some veterinary care."

"All right, okay," Freeman says.

Daddy takes the cage from Freeman and sets it on the floor. They say goodnight and Freeman leaves.

"Where are you going to put her for the night?" Daddy asks Mommy.

"Well, first, I think I'll get her out of that cage and into a carrier," Mommy says. "And then I'll put her in the guest bath downstairs, under the heat lamp to keep her warm."

"Are you going to do anything else for her tonight?" Daddy asks.

"There's nothing much I can do right now," Mommy tells

him. "As long as she's unconscious, I guess we'll have to assume that she's not suffering. I can also call our vet in the morning to see what she thinks."

"Good idea," says Daddy. "I'll see you upstairs—don't stay up too much later with her!"

"I won't," Mommy says, kissing Daddy goodnight.

I wait on the sofa as Mommy goes to the garage and returns with a carrier. She sets it next to me. Gently, she moves my mother from the cage into the carrier, cradling her head and body.

Mommy picks up the carrier, but not by the strap, the way she carries the boys. She bends to put her arms underneath the carrier and lifts it, supporting my mother and holding her steady. As she settles the carrier in the length between her elbows and wrists, I throw myself at it, trying to reach its top. I almost make it. My claws catch the soft webbing just below the carrier's roof, and I hang on, trying to scramble up as Mommy stops moving. "Lucy!" Mommy says. "If you want to come with us, you can." She waits while I settle myself. The roof of the carrier sags below my weight. I can feel my mother's warmth beneath me as Mommy cradles us both against her chest and walks to the downstairs guest room. She places the carrier on the floor of the bathroom and twists a knob on the wall. The lamp overhead begins to glow dimly, like an awakening sun. "That will warm it up in here soon, and I've set the timer for all night long," Mommy tells me. "I'll be back in a minute."

When Mommy returns with small bowls of food and water, I am lying on the tile beside my mother. "Oh, Lucy, are you going to keep her company?" she asks me.

I meow: yes.

"Well, that's fine," Mommy says. "Let me get one more thing."

This time, she is carrying a small litter box when she

returns. She sets it in a corner of the bathroom. Then she unzips the carrier, letting its door fall down and lie flat against the floor.

"I'll let you stay in here with her tonight, Lucy," Mommy says. "And I won't close the bathroom door, just the bedroom door—in case you want to walk around," she explains. "I'll be here very early in the morning to check on both of you—that's just a few hours from now, it's so late already!" she adds, looking at her watch. Then she leans down and kisses me goodnight. "And goodnight to you," she whispers to my mother, patting her head.

After Mommy leaves, I crawl into the carrier. I lie on my side, facing my mother, and drape my leg over her shoulders. I lick her face: first her eyes, then her nose, then the roots of her whiskers. Her breathing feels light on my face, like the most delicate of breezes, barely there.

I snuggle in against her belly, just as I did when I was a kitten. Back then, her belly was so hollow that I could feel her bones when I nursed. Now, it is plump and rounded, soft as a pillow. I press my face to her chest, craving the sound of her heartbeat. Its thumping feels far away and slow.

A halo of light begins to grow around us, as the lamp overhead glows brighter. The bathroom is heating up. My mother breathes a little more deeply, and I move slightly away from her rising and falling belly, so that I am next to her, pressing my nose against hers. I lay my paws on top of hers and flex my pads, holding on. My eyelids grow heavy with the warmth and cadence of my mother's breath, and I doze. In my dream, I am with my littermates once again, and we are sheltered against our mother's body, all of us entwined in a mass of lightly snoring fur.

I am shaken out of my unconscious purring: it is my mother, shuddering. Her eyes are open; they look hungry, just as I remember. But the hunger is for me: my mother's eyes are devouring my face. I feel them travel from my nose to the ends of my whiskers. They move up my cheeks and trace my eyes. Does she see the same dark outline that surrounds her eyes, I wonder? They rest on my ear, studying its notch. When my mother's eyes return to mine, I stare into their darkness, then lower my eyelids and open them slowly. My mother does not return the gesture. Her eyes stay wide and unblinking as she edges her face still closer to mine. She gasps as she opens her mouth and licks my nose. Her tongue is drier and rougher than I remember. A feeble purr rumbles in her throat.

I am opening my mouth to return her caress when my mother is seized by a tremor that seems to start from somewhere deep in her belly and moves along her body, more quickly than a wave breaking and rippling until it washes out on the shore. First her stomach quivers, and then her chest heaves. Her tail flops up and down. Her legs twitch, first her hind legs, and then her front ones. The muscles in her neck jump. Her head jerks upward and then falls to the floor of the carrier.

Startled, I pull myself up to look at her. My mother's eyes are still wide open, but they are empty now, staring. They no longer see me. Her mouth is ajar, but her tongue is still. I press my nose to hers, and hold my breath, to feel hers, warm on my face. There is none. A sudden, sharp pain shoots into my chest, like the single thrust of a vicious fang. I exhale, winded by its sting.

When Mommy comes for us, I am draped over my mother, trying to warm her cooling body. The dusty scent of her is fading. The lamp has lost its glow.

"Oh Lucy, what's happened?" Mommy says, reaching in the carrier for me, lifting me out and kissing me. She sets me down and reaches in for my mother. She sits on the floor, my mother in her lap. She pets her face, traces the sand dollar on her cheek, runs her finger along the dark edging of her eyes. "Lucy," she says. "This is your mother, isn't it, darling?"

I meow: yes.

"Oh, I am so sorry," Mommy says. She swallows hard and blinks her eyes. Her lashes grow damp. She feels along my mother's spine, and tenderly turns her on her back. She looks in between her paw pads, feels along her legs. She probes her stomach with her fingers. "I still can't feel anything broken or obvious," she tells me. "She must have an injury that we can't see, maybe internal bleeding or something, Lucy girl. I'm sorry that I couldn't have done more—but with no vet on the island except for when we do TNR, there aren't many choices. I doubt that the human doctor could have done anything to save her, if she was hurt this badly. But maybe I should have woken him up last night, just in case. I'm terribly sorry, sweetheart."

Mommy reaches up and pulls a towel off a rack beside the shower. She spreads the towel on the floor and lays my mother on top of it. She arranges her body like a sleeping cat: she turns my mother on her side and carefully tucks her into a ball, her front legs under her back ones until all the paws are in a clump. She picks up her chin and delicately places it on top of the paws. Then she lifts my mother's tail and uses it to encircle her legs, tucking its tip beneath her nose. She closes my mother's eyelids, first one and then the other, and then she strokes her head, one last time.

Mommy wraps the towel around my mother's body and stands up, holding her. "We'll bury her beside your deck, Lucy," she tells me, "right next to your favorite scaevola bush. And we'll get a beautiful marker for her grave, so that we can always remember where she is."

Mommy walks out of the bathroom. I know that she will be taking my mother to Tevin. I do not follow.

Later, when hunger finally motivates me to leave the guest room, its ache travels from my tummy to encircle my heart.

The boys are being zipped into their traveling bag. Frisco slinks to the back, where he hunkers down and hides behind Fred, who pokes his nose at the webbing, staring at me as I watch from across the room. I have failed again to keep my family with me.

Mommy walks toward me. She picks me up and kisses me. "Goodbye, Little Lucy," she says. "Please don't be too sad. We'll see you soon. You try to have fun with Tevin and Ginger!"

Daddy picks up the boys' traveling bag, turning to toss a "See you later, Lucy!" in my direction. Then, with a creak of the door, I am an orphan again.

I am home alone with Tevin and Ginger when I hear that someone very bad is coming—a visitor that no one wants.

"Frances is supposed to be here in four, five days," Tevin tells Ginger. "We must be ready."

The door opens and closes all day with people coming in and going out. Some of them are looking for Mommy and Daddy. Some are friends of Tevin and Ginger, neighbors and other workers on the island. More people than usual come by to borrow things: wood, hammers, nails. All of them talk about Frances.

"Are you going to stay on the island?" they ask each other.

"Anyone with any sense will leave," some say. "Frances could be much stronger by the time she gets here."

"I've been through worse, I'm staying," is the occasional answer, usually from one of the Bahamians. The paler people all seem to want to leave; some of them come by to ask whether they can catch a ride to Florida. When Tevin and

Ginger tell them that Mommy and Daddy aren't here, they chat nervously about making other plans. It's only a few of the darker, Bahamian people who are not afraid of Frances.

"Someone has to stay," the Bahamian named Dillon says, laughing his booming loud laugh that used to frighten me so, a laugh that fills up the house and bounces off the ceiling. "I be here to run everybody else out to the airport," he adds.

There is a lot of talk about boats, airplanes, ways of getting off the island and where to go.

"I hope Island Air adds extra flights," someone says.

"Onyx is still charging a hundred fifty dollars for a boat run to Bimini!" one of the Bahamians says, annoyed. "You'd think that when his own people need to get off, he'd lower the rate."

"No, not Onyx," comes the answer. "He won't miss a chance to make some money."

"Do you think Nassau will be safe?" Ginger asks, concerned.

"No, you should get your family out of the Bahamas altogether," a visitor answers. "No telling where Frances will turn."

"I will go to Miami," Tevin says. "Maybe she won't go there."

From underneath the sofa, I listen to the humans, the dreadful shudders in their voices making my own skin twitch underneath my fur, as though a huge dog were lurking just around the corner, waiting to pounce.

Freeman looks especially shaken when he comes to visit. "Uberan is leaving," he tells Ginger.

"Well, most folks are," Ginger says.

"No, no, I mean leaving the island altogether," Freeman tells her. "He's selling his house."

"Really?" Ginger asks. "He be that worried about Frances?"

"I don't know how afraid he is of Frances—he don't say

much, you know. Just told me he's had enough and he's putting the house up for sale. He's moving to Alaska."

"Alaska!" Ginger exclaims. "Isn't it *cold* in Alaska?"

"That's what I hear. But the weather will probably suit him fine—he's always hiding from the sun."

Tevin walks in and joins the conversation. "There aren't many people in Alaska, either, are there?"

"I don't believe so," Freeman answers him. "He can build himself a cabin out in the wilderness and sit in the dark, all alone."

Tevin chuckles. "Good riddance!" he says.

Freeman cracks a small smile. I realize that the fur has risen along my spine and my ears are angled back against my head.

Ginger looks concerned. "But what will *you* do?" she asks Freeman.

"I don't know," he says. "Look around, I guess, see if I can take on some work at another house. Or maybe the new owners will hire me. It will probably be a while until his place sells, anyway."

"Yeah, depending on what Frances does," Tevin says. "You might have plenty of cleaning up to do. But I've been thinking we could use another yardman around here. We just got that lot across the street, you know, and I am getting tired, man, taking care of all that by myself. I'll talk to Ray and Darcie about whether they could hire you."

"All right, all right!" Freeman perks up. "That would be great!"

I feel as though that dog is now breathing down my neck. Frances is so scary that *Uberan* is leaving! But at least, from what Tevin said, the other humans are planning to be around after Frances is gone. Maybe she only comes after bad people.

Then they start barring the doors and windows. "You stay

inside, Lucy," Tevin tells me. "We are closing up the house and you must not go outside, or you might get locked out there when Frances comes."

I pace from room to room, following Tevin and Ginger as they go to every door and window, covering them with sheets of dull crinkled metal that blocks out the view and lets in no light. When they're done, I can no longer see outside at all. The inside of the house is very dark. The only doors that are still open are the outside garage doors. Golf carts pull in and out, as visitors check on the humans or announce their own plans.

"I got a flight to the states, and I've come to wish you well," a man says.

"We've arranged a charter, do you want to go?" another asks. "There are empty seats, and we're taking our housekeeper with us."

"No, I am going to Nassau," Ginger answers, calm and determined.

"I am going to Florida," Tevin answers.

"What about me?" I wonder. Why does no one ask about me? Are they all going to go away and leave me locked inside this house, hoping that Frances can't get to me through the metal? I am so frightened that I don't even want to eat; I can barely force myself to the litter box.

As many sunrises as there are food bowls in the laundry room have passed since the talk about Frances started, and now my ears stand up with a sudden rush of hope: Daddy arrives. I hear his voice as soon as he walks through the creaking door. "Hey there, Tevin," he says. "Are we all set?"

"Yes sir," Tevin answers. "The storm shutters are closed, the outside furniture is stacked in the garage, and I cut the coconuts out of the trees. All we have to do is turn off the water and the power and we're ready to go!"

"Good, good," says Daddy. "Let me take a look around.

And how about you, Ginger? Are you sure you don't want to come to Florida? It looks as though you would be safe there. We'd be happy to take you."

"No, no," Ginger answers, in her careful, unwavering way. "I am going to Nassau."

"Frances could pass right over Nassau," Daddy warns. "You know that, right?"

"Yes, yes," Ginger answers. "I'm not worried. I have been through Andrew, you know."

"Okay, then," Daddy answers. "I wish I could change your mind, but you're a big girl!"

Ginger laughs, and Daddy and Tevin walk out into the garage.

"What about your *little* girl?" I wish I could ask, my heart falling with a thud to the bottom of my chest. Daddy doesn't even inquire about me or call my name or look for me. Is he going to leave me here alone, waiting for Frances?

I scurry to the garage door, lift my head, and meow at the door handle as loudly as I can, hoping that Daddy or Tevin will hear me from the other side. But instead, their voices fade into silence as they walk out of the garage and around the back of the house.

Frantic now, I run for the back wall, jumping onto the window ledges, screaming at the impassive metal coverings. Between my wails, I listen, hoping Daddy has heard me. But I hear nothing. Again and again, I cry out. Every time, my cries are greeted by the cold, gloomy silence of the shuttered windows.

Even Ginger, still inside the house, ignores me as she works steadily in the kitchen, picking up dishes and utensils from the counters and securing them behind cabinet doors.

I move from room to room, and when I reach the furthest room downstairs, my cries still unanswered, I seek shelter in a familiar spot: behind a low sofa bed that backs up to the beach wall, where I hid when I was first in the house. I hunker down, smelling my kitten smell still on the sofa back, seeing remnants of my kitten fur still clinging to its fabric.

I sit there, wondering. Windows covered, coconuts taken from trees, furniture brought in from the beach, humans fleeing the island...will I be safe in the house? Will anyone feed me? I have begun to feel quite sorry for myself when I hear Daddy's voice. "Lucy Belle," he hollers.

I don't make him call again. I wiggle out from my hiding place and sprint into the kitchen, meowing and looking up at Daddy.

"There's my little girl," he says. "You're coming to Florida with me, little Lucy," he whispers into my ear, carrying me into the TV room and gently setting me inside a traveling bag.

I am so relieved that I don't meow or purr or even try to lick Daddy's hand. I just fling myself deep into the bag. It is smaller than Fred and Frisco's, and does not smell like cat. I lie down, looking through the front, the way Fred does. It's like looking through a cobweb. I watch as Daddy says goodbye to Ginger—"and good luck!" he tells her. "Let us hear from you as soon as Frances is over."

"Okay," Ginger answers. "Goodbye, Tevin," she says. "Goodbye, Lucy."

"Goodbye, Gin," Tevin says, and then Daddy picks up my traveling bag and puts it over his shoulder. I sway with the bag, just as a boat sways on the water, rocked from side to side as Daddy walks through the creaking door and toward the golf cart.

"Don't forget to close the shutters over the garage doors when you leave the island," Daddy tells Ginger.

"No, no, I won't," Ginger assures him, as Tevin climbs

onto the back seat of the golf cart, and Daddy puts me down on the seat beside him, facing front.

Then the cart is moving, out of the garage and around my deck and down the driveway past my scaevola, from where I have watched so many golf carts go by. A small stone cross marks the spot where my mother is buried. I have lain in that spot many times. I meow softly, toward the cross. I hope that my mother is resting peacefully beneath it, still curled in a cozy ball. I know that she can't hear me, but it makes me feel better to say goodbye.

As we pick up speed, my body vibrates with the cart. We turn out of the driveway and go faster and faster down the road, the wind blowing harder than I have ever felt it, whipping into my eyes and forcing me to blink furiously. We drive away from our end of the island, past houses, trees and open spaces that I have never seen before. Here is a cat feeder, a tail hanging out of it, cats lined up beside it waiting their turns. Will Frances come for them?

Over a big hill, just off the road and high on a concrete pad, sit a pair of feeders. Cats are bunched around them, cats with markings like mine, the colors of sand and dirt. I strain to see through the webbing as Daddy stops to talk to a dark man walking up the hill.

"Are you staying for the hurricane, Jasper?" he asks the man.

Hurricane! I think. Of course! Hurricanes can flatten houses and lead Bahamians to tie themselves to trees. Naturally, the storms have names; humans like to name everything: themselves, animals, their golf carts, their boats—even their houses have names on my island.

"Oh, yes," Jasper answers, with a low, warm chuckle. "I've seen enough hurricanes—this one is going to be a baby."

"I hope you're right," answers Daddy.

"Would you mind taking a couple of packages to Florida for me?" Jasper asks. "I have some things I want to get to my daughter in Lauderdale."

"No problem," Daddy tells him. "Where are they?"

"Right here in the dormitory, waiting for a ride!" Jasper chuckles. His dark face crinkles with his smile.

"Okay—Tevin, come help me grab them," Daddy says. "Lucy girl, you stay put. We'll be right back." He walks away with Tevin and Jasper toward a long stucco building where some of the island workers live. It is studded with boarded-up windows. Over his shoulder, a cat jumps from the concrete pad onto the scrub grass below, stopping to gnaw at one of her hind paws, doubtless to remove a burr. Another cat strolls up and rubs himself against her.

I blink to clear my watery eyes and press my nose into an opening of the crisscrossed threads, trying to get a clearer view. The male is the color of sand with patches of dirt, like me. Stripes twirl up his tail like a snake. One of the female's eyes is outlined in dark fur, like mine. A familiar sand dollar dots her cheek. She stops gnawing at her paw and turns to rub her scent glands along the male cat.

My siblings, I think. Mommy would call them "little Lucys." But they are the offspring of my mother—her bloodlines run through our island—and they are strong and beautiful. I meow as loudly as I can, calling them to me.

"You're welcome!" Daddy yells, and my siblings scamper as he and Tevin begin to walk toward the golf cart. My meow blows away on the wind, unheard by my sister and brother, its meaning mistaken by Daddy.

"It's okay, Lucy girl," he answers me, setting a box on the back of the cart. "I'll take care of you." He sets the golf cart in motion again, down the hill. The marina is in front of us now, but there are very few boats. I guess they have all run from

Frances, carrying humans to safety.

My siblings cannot get away. They have no humans to pack them into a traveling bag and take them to shelter. But my mother, I remind myself, showed us a multitude of hiding places away from the whims of weather. My brother and sister will remember her lessons, just as I do. They will feel the wind picking up and see the sky going dark, and they will find a conduit or a cistern or even a cement building, if they're lucky, and they'll crawl inside and lie low until Frances does her dirty work and blows on by. My siblings are survivors, just as I am.

Daddy circles the marina and drives onto a narrow stretch of land: the airport, where we used to watch the humans' big birds—the island airplanes—take off and land, their wings not flapping, their round feet whining as they ground to a halt just before reaching the open water. One of those big birds sits there now, striped with the colors of the sea and sunset. Daddy parks the golf cart as a man walks toward us.

"Hey Leo," Daddy says. "We all set to go?"

"Yep, just give me your departure cards and I'll get us out of here," Leo answers.

Daddy and Tevin reach into their pockets and pull out folded papers, handing them to Leo, who takes a few steps onto the porch of a tiny building at the edge of the airport. His hair whips in the wind; he hunches his shoulders against its bluster. When Leo reaches the door of the building, he does not duck inside for shelter—instead, he abruptly steps back. In the doorframe appears a human unlike any I have ever seen. Strips of cloth encircle his head, from beneath the collar of his tightly buttoned shirt to the brim of his wide, stiff hat, fastened with a string beneath his chin. The cloths appear to cover his entire face. His arms are hidden by billowing shirt-sleeves. Below them hang swollen hands that look way too big for his body, like the paws of a full-grown tomcat attached to a newborn kitten. They are the color of freshly cooked lobsters, but shinier. The man holds his hands out and away from his body, his arms stiff like malformed branches that have grown away from a tree trunk, aiming for the ground rather than the sky.

The man wears baggy shorts made of flimsy fabric that flap in the breeze, slapping against more cloths. These cloths look thicker than the ones on his face and stretch from underneath his shorts all the way to his ankles, where they disappear inside boots that look somehow familiar. I strain against my bag, trying to focus my bleary eyes. The man hobbles rigidly through the door of the building and onto the porch, his steps as slow as a hermit crab's exploring the edge of a concrete wall, cautiously feeling its way so as not to fall off. "Who in the heck is that?" Daddy asks Tevin.

"That," answers Tevin, "is our buddy Uberan." He laughs, low and a little bit mean. "Looks like he didn't head to Alaska quite soon enough."

"What in the world happened to him?" Daddy asks.

"Had to board up his house himself," Tevin answers. "Freeman took off for Andros to be with his family, Mosey's gone, and nobody else left around here wanted to help the rascal. So near as we can figure, Uberan worked all by himself yesterday, sunup to sundown, hauling and hammering, trying to save his big old place from Frances so that he can sell it. Just one thing he forgot in his big old hurry: sunscreen!" This time, Tevin's laugh sounds like the cackle of a satisfied hen who has just laid a humongous egg. "Jasper says the island doc was up all night, trying to get the swelling down and wrapping those bandages all over him. Says Uberan cried like a baby a couple o' times, the pain was so bad. Says even the tears hurt his cheeks!"

"Well, lucky for Uberan that the doctor hadn't evacuated

yet, I guess," Daddy says. He pulls the golf cart forward, until its nose is practically resting on the porch where Uberan stands awkwardly, teetering in the wind.

"Mr. Uberan!" Daddy calls. "Can we give you a ride somewhere?"

Uberan picks up a foot and thrusts it forward, toward us. The effort looks slow and torturous, like a conch inching along an unexpected sandbar. He lifts the other foot and advances, planting his legs far apart from each other. The space between them is wide open like the pliers Tevin uses in the garage. As he marches gingerly toward our cart, I can see bubbles on his hands that appear to be filled with water, as plentiful as knobs on a starfish. And there are cutouts in the cloths that cover his face. Tiny slits expose his eyes. Open circles allow just enough room for his nostrils. From a gash below them protrude what must be his lips. They look like a pair of obese earthworms, slimy and engorged with darkened blood.

When Uberan is almost next to Daddy, he stops. His lips do not move, but a noise comes out of his mouth, like a weak gust of wind. "Nuh," he says.

"Excuse me?" Daddy replies.

Uberan sucks in air; it whistles between his dreadful lips. "*Nuh!*" he says again, spitting the air back out.

"Oh!" Daddy answers. "I'm sorry, I didn't understand. Just looked like maybe you could use a ..."

Before Daddy can finish his sentence, a ribbon that holds the golf cart's rain cover in place breaks loose. At the end of the ribbon is a ridged metal snap. A blast of wind hurls the ribbon toward Uberan. The snap slams into his hand, smack in the middle of an enormous bubble. It bursts open like a coconut smashed with a sledgehammer. Water sprays onto the windshield. Drops settle onto the steering wheel. Daddy wipes his cheek. Uberan jerks backward, his arm swinging violently. A scream breaks out of his deformed mouth. "*Aarrrggghh!*" He rocks on his heels, then steadies himself. His chest heaves.

"Are you okay?" Daddy asks.

Uberan sucks in another breath and holds it. I watch his lips. They barely wriggle as he gasps out the answer. "Get *lost,*" he hisses. There is no mistaking the words, even on the hurricane wind. Daddy stares at him, speechless, then turns to look at Tevin. "Let's get out of here," Daddy says.

"All right, *okay!*" answers Tevin. "Somebody should put this creep on ice!" he says, right in front of Uberan. "What do they call those big blue slabs of ice in Alaska?"

"Glaciers," Daddy tells him.

"Right. Glaciers! Somebody should drop him on a glacier and let him chill out for good," Tevin snorts, looking straight at Uberan.

Daddy chokes down a laugh and concentrates on the steering wheel. He backs up the golf cart and parks it along a low slab of concrete. He swings my bag over his shoulder and walks toward the big waiting bird. I twist myself around and watch Uberan shuffle away, fascinated. His movements look so measured and painful that I feel a surprising stab of sympathy for him. But I bat the thought away like an irritating fly. He had no sympathy for my mother, lying in the road. I turn my back to Uberan and watch where I am going.

Daddy carries me up skinny stairs that lead from the ground to the bird's huge round belly. Inside, it looks like a house! The same soft stuff is on the floor, colored like the sea. There are the same cushy chairs, tables, and lots of windows.

"Welcome to RayDar Air, little Lucy," Daddy says, putting my bag in a chair next to a window, turning it so I can see outside. "You are on your way home."

Home. At last, I'm on my way to the place called Florida.

Daddy settles into a seat across from me. Leo comes in behind us, closes the heavy door, and climbs into a chair up in the beak, facing away from Daddy and me. Tevin is already sitting up there.

My head is spinning faster than the gigantic blades that suddenly come to life at the end of the beak, making a terrible racket and stirring up a gusty wind. The bird starts to move down the runway, slowly at first, then faster and faster. Just as we reach the water's edge, the bird throws itself into the air with a shriek, climbing for the clouds.

I look out my window, and there below is my island, a narrow strip of coral rock and grass dotted with scrub and trees, the flaming colors of tropical flowers and houses painted to match the bougainvillea and hibiscus—all sitting in the middle of sea and sand.

Higher and higher we go into the sky. I watch out my window, straining my neck to see, until my island fades away below me.

"Oh, Lucy girl, you made it!" Mommy says, holding her arms out for me. She is standing at the top of a short stairway behind a garage door in a house the color of sand and clouds. The door closes silently behind us. Mommy folds me against her chest and kisses my head. Then she kisses Daddy. "So, how did it go?" she asks.

"No problem," Daddy tells her. "We came through Fort Lauderdale and whisked her right through customs—no questions asked."

"Wonderful! I was so worried you wouldn't get through and would have to take her back to the island. Tomorrow first thing she'll get her papers from the vet. Then you won't be an illegal alien anymore, Lucy!" Mommy says, nuzzling my neck. "How did she do on the plane and in the car?"

"No problem there, either," says Daddy. "She didn't seem scared at all. She's a very adaptable little kitty. She rode on my shoulders, looking around."

I rub my nose on Mommy's, and she rubs mine back.

"That's good, because you are going to have a whole lot to get used to now," she says. "Planes and cars are just the beginning. Would you like a tour of your Florida house?"

As Mommy bends to put me on the floor, I hear the jangle of familiar bells. Fred comes loping down another staircase—a long, swirling one—and runs toward me, stopping a couple of cat lengths away to lift his nose in the air and sniff in my direction. He stares at me, wide-eyed, and I know he can't quite believe he is seeing me in this house. I stand still, returning his gaze for just a few breaths, and then I take the first step. I walk over and lift my nose in greeting. Fred thinks it over, and after several breaths, lowers his nose and touches mine—ever so briefly—before he twists and saunters into a big, open kitchen.

I follow deferentially, several steps behind him. Frisco rounds a tall counter, stopping in his tracks to look at me with the same disbelieving stare that Fred did. I immediately lie down, submissive, opening and closing my eyes slowly in a friendly greeting. Frisco raises his ears and tail, and strides toward me, his mouth open, his nose twitching. I lie still as a shell while he smells me from nose to haunches. When he finishes his sniffing, Frisco turns toward a bench in the corner. He leaps gracefully onto the bench and buries his face in a food bowl resting there, all in one easy, elegant movement. As I watch him, my stomach growls. I am hungry again—for the first time in several sunrises. And then I notice that there is a bowl on either side of Frisco, filled with food. A bowl for Frisco, a bowl for Fred, a bowl for...me? The other bowl must be for me!

I measure the distance from floor to bench with my eyes,

sizing it up as carefully as I can. I decide to aim for the bowl that looks just a hair further from Frisco than the other. I sink back on my haunches, stiffen my whiskers, propel myself off the ground, and land on the bench with barely a wobble! Frisco keeps on eating, not deigning to look up at me. I move toward my chosen bowl, tentatively. When I am shoulder to shoulder with Frisco, I crouch in front of the bowl and slowly move my face toward it. My tongue hangs out in anticipation, but I halt in mid-movement as Frisco jerks his head up and stares at me straight in the eyes. I lower my lashes. Frisco reaches over and taps my nose with his—just one light, brusque touch. He goes back to his eating, ignoring me. I plunge my mouth into the food. A purr leaps into my throat of its own accord.

This is home.

I have arrived.

Postscript

I hear the humans say that cats have nine lives.

They say this when Fred falls overboard and swims back to the boat, climbing safely aboard and looking like a newborn rat. They say it when Frisco calls out from the air conditioning vent where, hiding as he likes to, he has been trapped when the handyman covers the hole with wood. They say it about me—and now that you have read my story, you know why.

Nine lives is one less claw than I have on my two front paws. I figure I've lived just over one paw's worth of lives so far, and who knows what other adventures await me?

Mommy says my next life could be as an "animal welfare advocate," just like she is. She tells me that my book will fetch human money, and that we will use some of it to help other animals, which is one of the things she likes to do with money.

Mommy says if we could become a world of compassion, not cruelty, everyone could have a life like mine. She says we wouldn't hurt or kill each other—we'd all help each other.

Then she kisses me on top of my head, and I lick her nose, and I think that kind of world sounds yummy.

Love and compassion to all of you,

Lucy Miracle

◇◇◇◇◇◇◇◇◇

If you'd like to help the animals yourself, you can start with:

The Humane Society of the United States: www.hsus.org

Farm Sanctuary: www.farmsanctuary.org

Tell them Lucy sent you!

Author's Note

A word on feral/community cats: reasonable minds differ on whether humans should attempt to tame feral cats. I believe that the decision depends on the cat and the situation. I know many formerly feral cats who are now among the most loving members of their human households, Lucy included. I also know (from a distance) many feral cats who apparently want no contact with humans. And while I cannot speak with authority for every feline, I do not believe that a cat would exert as much energy as Lucy does in this story, when trying to find her biological mother. Lucy's search is part of the fun of fiction.

For more information on Trap Neuter Return, check the links on www.cathyunruh.com.

Acknowledgements

Thank you to the friends who critiqued Lucy's story when it was nothing but words spilled on paper: Caren Lobo, Ellen McVay, and Mike Dunn, who carefully reviewed several iterations.

Nancy Trichter generously shepherded the project as it became a book and introduced me to my first editor, Gretchen Salisbury.

Gene Baur, Jim MacDougald, Nancy McCall, Dennis McCullough, Rory Freedman, Margo Hammond, Tara Hood, Bryan Kortis, Myriam Parham, Sherry Silk, and Loretta Swit all endorsed the early manuscript. Thanks to each of you for your faith.

Nancy Peterson, a mentor and angel with the Humane Society of the United States, connected me with Collage Books. My editor there, Sandra Yeyati, is meticulous and creative. Publisher Jeff Hirsch, of Collage, is passionate not only about books, but about cats. My publicist, Marie Hamm, is tireless and talented.

Our beloved housekeeper, Dorothy Sturrup, cares for our human family and our felines. All of us are thankful for Dorothy's presence in our lives. She helps to make the Bahamas beautiful.

And what would I do without girlfriends? Especially the ones who first loved Lucy: Sue Green, Elaine Kaufman, Alyce McCathran, Michele Phillips, Eileen Rodriguez and Linda Steele.

My deepest love and gratitude to God, through whom all things are possible, and to my husband Tom, without whom this story would not have been possible.

About the Author

Cathy Unruh is an Emmy Award winning television journalist and a longtime animal advocate. She grew up on a hobby farm, where the interaction with cats, dogs, rabbits, horses, sheep, and cows taught her that animals are individuals, not commodities.

Unruh resides in the Tampa Bay area of Florida, where she is also active in a number of causes benefiting humans. Since the writing of this book, she, her husband Tom, and their cats Fred, Frisco, and Lucy have been joined by Wee Willie Winky, a Shih Tzu rescued from a puppy mill.